LP REMINGT

Remington, Henry.
Man called Slaughter :
Henry Remington.

ATCHISON PUBLIC LIBRARY
401 Kansas
Atchison, KS 66002

ATCHISON LIBRARY
401 KANSAS
ATCHISON, KS 66002

SPECIAL MESSAGE TO READERS

This book is published under the auspices of
THE ULVERSCROFT FOUNDATION
(registered charity No. 264873 UK)

Established in 1972 to provide funds for research, diagnosis and treatment of eye diseases. Examples of contributions made are: —

- A Children's Assessment Unit at Moorfield's Hospital, London.

- Twin operating theatres at the Western Ophthalmic Hospital, London.

- A Chair of Ophthalmology at the Royal Australian College of Ophthalmologists.

- The Ulverscroft Children's Eye Unit at the Great Ormond Street Hospital For Sick Children, London.

You can help further the work of the Foundation by making a donation or leaving a legacy. Every contribution, no matter how small, is received with gratitude. Please write for details to:

THE ULVERSCROFT FOUNDATION,
The Green, Bradgate Road, Anstey,
Leicester LE7 7FU, England.
Telephone: (0116) 236 4325

In Australia write to:
THE ULVERSCROFT FOUNDATION,
c/o The Royal Australian College of Ophthalmologists,
27, Commonwealth Street, Sydney, N.S.W. 2010.

A MAN CALLED SLAUGHTER

Beautiful Rose Turner runs a ranch north of the Rio Diablo in Arizona and is courted by handsome Mexican Jesus Serrano, who reigns over his hacienda on the far side of the river. But when Rose discovers the Mexican's vicious nature, she ends the courtship. Jesus retaliates by running off with her cattle and poisoning her wells, leaving Rose with little choice but to hire the laconic bounty hunter Slaughter. Soon the body count is rising as Slaughter's weapons roar . . .

HENRY REMINGTON

A MAN CALLED SLAUGHTER

Complete and Unabridged

LINFORD
Leicester

First published in Great Britain in 1999 by
Robert Hale Limited
London

First Linford Edition
published 2000
by arrangement with
Robert Hale Limited
London

The moral right of the author
has been asserted

Copyright © 1999 by Henry Remington
All rights reserved

British Library CIP Data

Remington, Henry
 A man called Slaughter.—Large print ed.—
Linford western library
1. Western stories
2. Large type books
I. Title
823.9'14 [F]

ISBN 0–7089–5790–0

Published by
F. A. Thorpe (Publishing)
Anstey, Leicestershire

Set by Words & Graphics Ltd.
Anstey, Leicestershire
Printed and bound in Great Britain by
T. J. International Ltd., Padstow, Cornwall

This book is printed on acid-free paper

1

'Life is a whore's promise.' The *hombre*'s face beneath the shadow of his wide-brimmed hat was deeply rutted like carved wood. He was lounging with his viciously rowelled, dust-white boots up on a spare chair. 'Thass all it is.'

The young dude at the bar turned to give him the once-over. 'I don't believe I was talking to you.'

'You asked what the hell life is all about. So, I'm telling you.' The man's lips beneath a thick moustache, above a grey-stone jaw, hardly moved as he spoke. There was something atavistic, touched by the blood of the Indian, about his face. Only the green eyes moved, lizard-like, venomous. 'Keep your questions to yourself, mister, if you don't want a reply.'

The dude, with his slicked-back hair smelling strongly of macassar-oil, and in his go-to-church clothes, smiled widely. 'So, we have a philosopher among us? Why so cynical, friend? Has life dealt you a bad hand, too?'

It occurred to him to say that judging from the stranger's get-up it had. The tattered range leathers, the greasy bandanna knotted about his strong throat, the sweat-smelling shirt that looked like it hadn't been washed in weeks. But the heavy Schofield revolver slung across the man's loins deterred him from being too frank.

'Maybe it has, maybe it hasn't. But there ain't no point in griping.' The saddle bum lifted the bottle of skull-crush whiskey to his mouth, and his Adam's apple jerked twice as he swallowed. 'So why don't you shut up? I ain't int'rested in hearing 'bout your troubles; I got enough of my own.'

'Again I should point out, friend, that I was not addressing you. I was in conversation with Charley here.' The young man nodded at the bar-keep. 'Surely I am allowed to discuss the problems of the day over a drink? He asked me how I was.'

'That was just him being polite. That don't mean he wants to hear all the pig-swill. Nor me, neither.'

Again the young gent, in his broad-striped frocksuit and bowstring tie, smiled with amusement. 'I fear the whiskey makes you truculent, but that is no reason to pick an argument with me.'

The other occupants of the long, bare-boarded saloon — three shabby men flicking cards across a table at the far end, a couple of *nymphs du prairie* flopped out on a horsehair sofa nearby, the paint on their faces clammy in the heat — showed little interest in the altercation. Only the barman's hooded eyes studied the vagrant. He had drifted in a few hours before from out of the Arizona desert. God alone knew where from. But he had trouble written all over him.

'I ain't picking an argument with you.' There was a flicker of mockery on the *hombre*'s lips. '*Why*? You lookin' for one?'

'No.' The slim young man put a shiny boot on the footrail and turned his back deliberately on him. 'Nor do I give a rat's ass for your philosophy.'

'Rat's ass?' the drifter muttered, pulling the Schofield from its greased holster. 'Where's he get off talking this fancy way?'

The 'keep's dark pupils dilated as he stared at the revolver, and he gave the youngster a significant glance, reaching to pat his hip, slowly. The dude nodded, and his shoulders tensed under the suit.

The stone-faced rolled the cylinder of the pistol, first one way, then the other. At each turn it clicked twice. There was a pause, then it clicked twice again. The only other sounds in the saloon were of a fly buzzing and the men at the far end murmuring over their cards. The drifter gripped the revolver butt with his right hand, aiming it vaguely at the street, and with his left thumb spun the cylinder full round, like a casino wheel.

The sound of the cylinder was both an irritant and a threat to the two men at the bar. Their faces had become stern. The 'keep backed away to one side and begun to absentmindedly polish glasses, listening to the clicking, the clicking away of seconds to what must surely be a gun duel. He glanced at his 12-gauge beneath the counter.

The young man spun back to face his tormentor, the fingers of his hands outstretched at his hips, a strand of his greasy hair fallen over one eye. 'Look, what do you want? What have I done to you? If it's a gunfight you want I'm ready whenever you are.' He slowly unbuttoned his jacket skirts, and swung them aside to reveal a pair of ivory-handled Remingtons holstered butts forward on each hip. 'Just say when, mister.'

The hewn face was immobile, framed by thick black hair hanging almost to his shoulders as it studied the

Schofield, and he clacked the cylinder shut. There was a scoffing gasp of laughter, and he shrugged as he looked up and met the youngster's eyes. 'Am I botherin' you?'

'Yes, you are. Who are you? What's your name? I like to know who a man is if I'm going to kill him.'

'An optimist, eh?' The down-at-heel stranger gave another scoffing laugh deep in his throat, which sounded more like a snake's rattle warning of attack. 'Look, mister, if I'm talking to a man, I don't like him to turn his back. Who are *you*? You tell me who you are and I might tell you who I am.'

'The handle's Ben Turner. I run the Mexican Hat Ranch, fifteen miles out of town. Yes, you are getting on my nerves. I don't wish to kill you, but I've had enough of drunken riff-raff mongrels chewin' at my heels.'

'Ha! Listen to him! You callin' me drunken riff-raff? Mister, them's fighting words.' The arrogantly lounging gunslinger still had his boots up on the chair, and leisurely adjusted his position, suddenly spinning the Schofield on one finger and pointing it at the ceiling. The youngster's shoulders and hands twitched in readiness, but the man only grinned at him, took another swig of the bottle. 'I must admit you got spunk. You don't look like no rancher to me.'

'And you don't look like no Sunday-school preacher. Well, I asked you a question?'

'Slaughter. James Slaughter. I'm a hunter by profession. I hunt men. Bounty hunter. But right now I'm resting. Maybe you need to hire me, Turner? Weren't you saying that somebody's poisoned your water? And don't tell me I shouldn't have been listening.'

'I don't need to hire a killer, thanks. I can handle my problems, myself.'

'It don't sound like you're being too successful.' James Slaughter sighed, and slapped at the big meaty fly that had landed on his bare wrist. It was a fast movement, squashing it. He wiped its blood and puss off on his leather chaps. 'Don't worry, I ain't gonna kill you. It's too hot. Not unless someone pays me to. So relax.'

Ben Turner smiled, and dropped his frock coat back across his guns. He picked up his glass and finished his drink. He looked at Slaughter and frowned. 'You mean nobody sent you? But if somebody paid you, you *would* try to shoot me?'

'Nothing personal. Only business.'

'How much do you charge as a hired gun?'

Slaughter studied what little was left of the whiskey. 'That depends. How long the job takes. How many men I have to put down. Generally, I ask five hundred down and five hundred on completion. That's when I ain't bounty-huntin'. And I ain't at this moment. The Fargo office ain't got nuthin' for me. I jest dropped them off a stage robber. Remember Jed Hanks? He'd been dead for days. Stunk like a dead cat. I been trailin' him a month. And all I got is four hundred lousy bucks. They gonna mail it to me. Sometimes, I can tell you, this rotten game jest ain't worth it.'

Turner looked at the bar-keep. 'You think he's tellin' the truth? Or is this whiskey talk?'

The barman shrugged. 'I seen him ride in earlier trailing a bronc with a stiff over it. He went into the Wells, Fargo office. So I guess he is.'

'Sch-whooooo!' Slaughter made an expression of disgust, cleared his throat, and spat. 'He sure did stink. Thass why I'm hittin' the whiskey. I don't usually take a whole bottle. It ain't good for the aim.' He put out his tongue to catch the last drip, stood, stretched, stuck the Schofield back in the holster, and slammed the empty bottle down on the bar. He picked up a striped blanket poncho and wheeled it around his shoulder. 'So, shall I be moseying on? Or — ? You still figure you can handle things yourself?'

When Turner did not reply, the bounty man slapped a silver dollar onto the bar, gave a wry smile and sauntered from the saloon, his Mexican spurs jangling. The men at the card table glanced up, uninterested, and, desultorily, dealt another hand. One of the prostitutes yawned, and hoicked her knee up showing her drawers. The 'keep wiped the bar, and tossed the empty bottle into a box. 'So long, Mr Turner. Hope you sort out your troubles. I think you're wise not to get mixed up with him.'

'Perhaps. *Adios*, Charley.' Ben Turner strode out into the blaze of sunlight. Down by the hitching rail, the *hombre* was standing, swaying slightly from the rotgut. He was tightening the cinch of a pinto. He put a boot-toe into the bentwood stirrup, a hand on the horn, and swung into the saddle, sitting straight-backed, wheeling the horse away.

Turner unhitched his own horse and rode after him. He caught up as they passed the water tower on the edge of the town. 'You want to ride out to the ranch?' he called.

'Sure,' Slaughter grunted, as if he had been expecting him. 'If you can pay my price. Remember I don't give no guarantees.'

'A month's trial. Five hundred down and five hundred at the end of thirty days.'

'Or however long it takes.'

The younger man leaned over and offered his hand. The gunman returned a firm grip.

'I guess I could use someone to watch my back.'

'It's a deal, *amigo*.'

2

There was a noticeboard nailed to a stake by the water-hole, the roughly painted warning, 'Poison', above a skull and crossbones for those who couldn't read. But the dead longhorns, rolled over, their hooves kicking air, as if still in the throes of agony, needed no words. There were two dozen of them or more, their putrefying flesh beginning to seethe with flies and maggots.

'They tipped a barrel of strychnine in.' Ben Turner stared at the desolate scene. 'Did it in the night. I never thought men could fall so low.'

'Man is the highest form of life on this earth,' Slaughter said, shaking his head as he sat his mustang. 'At least, thass what a preacher told me once. In my opinion he's gen'rally the lowest, lower than the snakes and serpents that crawl on their bellies. Nothing much surprises me no more. But this' — he pointed a gloved finger at the hole strung around now with barbed wire — '*this* is the lowest of the low.'

They rode on across the parched land, climbing up through a forest of great saguaro cactii, their arms raised heavenwards as if beseeching the blue heavens for rain.

'You have a very low opinion of man.'

'In my profession that comes with the job. I don't trust nobody and nuthin'. Why even these damn soo-aros are lying. They look dry but they got tons of water concealed inside. Their roots stretch out for a hundred paces or more.'

'I guess they've learned how to conceal the fact they can survive.'

'Mister, in these parts that's the secret of stayin' alive. You have to be tougher and craftier than your opposition; you have to be cunning; you have to adapt.'

'I've had the boys go through the brush and roust out any other cattle, drive them down to the river,' Ben said. 'With this drought that's only a trickle and we share it with him.'

'Him?'

'Yes, Jesus del Muchado Serrano. He owns the land on the other side, the Tejon Rancho.'

'Jesus!' Slaughter gave his scoffing throat gargle. 'They sure named him right.'

'I've no proof he did it, but it figures.'

'He covets your land?'

'No, I believe he covets my sister more than the land.'

'Your sister?'

'Yes, it was before I arrived here. I have been away for some years working in Kansas City. But I understand Rose was engaged to be married to Serrano. I know Dad didn't approve. Anyway something happened and she broke it off. Dad died suddenly of a heart attack last year, and Rose wrote and said she was having problems, so I came back to see what I could do.'

'Which was?'

'Not a lot. We tried to put a stop to the rustling. The cattle were obviously disappearing across the river onto Serrano's land. I rode across to try to reason with him. Nobody wants a range war. He, of course, denied all knowledge. He offered a ridiculous price to buy us out. He implied that our lives might be in danger if we did not accept. I told him to go to hell, do his worst.'

'And he did?'

'Well, nobody's gotten killed yet, except the livestock.'

They rode on in silence for a while through the harsh, dusty landscape until James Slaughter muttered, 'When a man's been flouted in love it can harden his heart. Especially a man of the proud Latin temperament like your friend Jesus.'

'He comes from an old aristocratic family, as his name implies, and he has inherited their arrogance, cruelty and vices, and few of their virtues. I believe Rose was misled by his courtly manners at first, before she discovered his true nature.'

'Intense love can turn into intense hatred,' the bounty hunter murmured, as if he knew this from first-hand experience. 'I guess he needs to humiliate her. From the sound of it, thangs can only git worse.'

'To tell you the truth,' Ben said, forcing a reckless grin. 'You threw a scare into me in the saloon. I thought he had sent you to kill me.'

'That's why you were so eager to face up to me?'

'Yes, it's not what I want, but I'm ready to go down shooting. I've always hated bullies. I'm not ready to be ridden over.'

'That why you left home? Your father bully you?'

'No, not really. He was a hard man, but just. He wanted to turn me into a carbon copy of himself, take over the reins of the ranch.' Ben Turner looked around at the bleak landscape, the strangely eroded red rocks, the plants all bearing barbs, claws and thorns. 'Would you want to live your life here? Mm, maybe you would. Me, I wanted to see more of the world.'

'So, what did you make of yourself?'

'I'm a newspaper writer. That's what I'm cut out for. Chasing cows all day ain't my cup of coffee.'

'A hack, a scribbler? Mighta guessed by the way you use them fancy words. No wonder you didn't see eye to eye with your daddy.'

'I'm pretty well respected in Kansas City in my line of work. I had no wish to come back here to all this . . . this trouble.'

'Only Rose won't budge?'

'That's true. I've urged her to sell up. But she's got an obstinate streak in her, like Dad.'

By this time they had sighted the cluster of plank buildings that was the Mexican Hat Ranch, set amidst a benchland of blue sage: corrals, forge, stables, bunkhouse, the ranch house set apart.

'Home sweet home, eh?' Slaughter grunted.

'Yes, you could say. Or it would be if it weren't for Jesus del Muchado Serrano and his boys.'

★ ★ ★

'Whoo!' James Slaughter gave a low whistle of appreciation as a young woman came out onto the porch of the ranch house. 'Some looker! I can see why Señor Serrano mighta been upset.' He clenched his fist, lasciviously, and thrust it. '*Whup-pah*! He let a worthy prize outa his grasp, eh?'

'I would rather you didn't talk about Rose like that,' Ben Turner said, in a lowered voice. 'I will trust you, while you are with us, to treat her with respect.'

'Aw, sure.' Slaughter gave his low cackle. 'I allus treat a lady with respect.

But that popgun she's carryin' ain't gonna keep her enemies at bay for long.'

Rose Turner had a slim-barrelled, single-shot sporting rifle in her hands as she stepped out. She was wearing a plain blue cotton summer frock with puffed half-sleeves, a scalloped neckline, but not immodestly low. She had shiny, raven-black hair like her brother, but her skin was luscently pale, an attribute much valued in this land of dark faces. And there was something of the aristocrat, too, about the haughty way she held her well-chiselled features.

An old guy busy repairing a wagon outside the forge had clanged a warning triangle when he saw the cloud of dust kicked up by the riders, and had come running across with a rifle in readiness to defend the ranch house, before he recognized Ben Turner.

'Hello.' Rose's voice had a bell-like clarity. 'How did it go?'

'Not too well.' Ben gave a shrug of

displeasure as he dismounted. 'Or as expected. Nobody wanted to know.'

'What? You saw the sheriff? Isn't he going to do anything?'

'The sheriff, the mayor, the banker, Doc Greaves, anyone who's anybody in San Andreas: they were all of the opinion this is something we have to settle for ourselves.'

'In other words they're all yaller.' Slaughter had stepped down from his mustang with a slow, deliberate kind of lithe grace with which he performed all his actions. 'They're all scared of risking their lousy lives to help a friend and neighbour.'

'Who's he?' Rose's nostrils twitched, fastidiously, as the ragged *hombre* joined them on the veranda and she caught a whiff of his aroma. 'A new hand?'

'No. This is James Slaughter. He will be staying with us a while.'

'Jeez, my head.' Slaughter took off his hat and wiped sweat from his brow, scraping fingers back through his thick, dusty hair. 'Feels like it's been kicked by a mule. That knock 'em dead's got a powerful punch. I sure could do with a strong mug of black cawfee.'

'James, this is my sister, Rose Turner.'

'Howdy. Some folks call me Stone-face Slaughter. And some have more colourful epithets, 'specially when I'm on their tail. But Jim'll do, seeing as we're gonna be thrown together for a while.'

Without invitation he walked into the house and looked around. The living-room was barely, but neatly furnished, showing a woman's touch in the colour of the curtains and the table covering. It was clean, but nothing could prevent the red dust from seeping through the doors and windows and settling on everything. Slaughter was not so much interested in artistic decor as the possibility of defending it from attack. He did not look too impressed.

Rose went into the kitchen, beckoning Ben with a jerk of her head. 'Who *is* he?' she hissed, as she put a big black kettle on the stove to boil. 'What is he doing here?'

'He's going to help us.'

'What that whiskey-breath? I don't like his attitude. Who does he think he is? How can he help us?'

'With his guns. Just fix the coffee, Rose. I'll explain in due course. We're in a desperate fix. You know that.'

'Guns — ?'

But Ben had returned to the other room to find the bounty hunter collapsed in the best armchair, his spurred boots up on a stool, his eyes closed.

'Jeez,' Slaughter whispered. 'Why do I do it?'

'Do what?'

'Drink?'

'Don't ask me.' Ben went to a corner safe, unlocked it, took out a cash box, counted out notes of varied denominations, shuffled them into a pile and was about to hand them to the gunman when Rose entered the room bearing a tray of cups and coffee pot. 'There you are,' Ben said, slapping the payment down on a low table.

'What on earth are you doing?' There was a shrill note of anger in Rose's voice. 'What are you giving away out money for? We're almost bankrupt as it is.'

'Don't worry, Rose, he ain't lost it to me at poker,' Slaughter muttered. 'It's like a down payment on my services. Regard me as a knight in shinin' armour, here to rescue a lady in distress.'

'What?' The cups and saucers rattled as Rose crashed them down onto the table. 'What do you mean?'

'Waal, look at it t'other way: he's hired me to do yuh killin' fer yuh, seein' as you ain't up to it.'

'Killing? We don't want any killing.'

'Seems to me a gun's the only way you gonna stop 'em runnin' you off this land. Killin's the only way, Rose. It's the only language they understand.'

'Ben, I want that money back. Get

this man out of here.'

James Slaughter was calmly counting it through. He held it up. 'Make your mind up, Ben. I hope you ain't wasted my time. Who wears the pants in this house?'

'You rude, insolent, smelly, horrible person. Return that money, drink up your coffee and get out of my house. I'm sorry you've been troubled. Ben's made a mistake.'

Slaughter kept hold of the money, as she reached out to take it and it seemed like they might have a little tug-of-war with the cash. 'Ben ain't made a mistake: it's you's making the mistake, lady. From what I hear and see of thangs some drastic remedy is required. I'm prepared to put my life on the line and, maybe, be that remedy. But, I don't do that 'less I git paid. Right?'

Rose slowly released the notes and sank back onto a chair. She put her fingers to her forehead, staring at the puma-skin carpet on the floorboards.

'Oh, my God,' she whispered. 'I never thought it would come to this. That we would have to pay a hired killer.'

'We've got to do it, Rose. I ain't no match for them on my own. And the boys, those that haven't already been run off, they're just ordinary ranch-hands. We need his help.'

'You think so?'

'There's always the possibility, if we don't employ him, that Mr Slaughter might go and join Serrano.'

The girl looked up, her vivid violet eyes meeting the flickering, lizard-like green ones in the hard face. 'You wouldn't?'

'Waal, I gotta make a living, lady.' He held the wad of cash out, mockingly. 'Mebbe Serrano wouldn't be so reluctant to take me on.' When she did not reply, he tucked the cash into his shirt pocket. 'So, how about that cawfee?'

As if in a trance she poured a cup of the steaming black liquid, and her hand trembled as she passed it across, making the cup chatter in the saucer.

'I hope you ain't gonna be nervous of me, Rose. Or stay angry, whatever it is making you spill this.' He tipped the spilt coffee in the saucer back in the cup. 'I may be a bit rough in my manners, but you'll soon git used to me.'

'I sincerely hope not. You are not a man I would want to get used to. And, for a start, you can get this clear, I am not having you sleeping in this house. You can go over into the bunkhouse with the other men. And eat with them, too.'

'Waal!' There was a humorous flicker to the gunman's lips. 'That ain't friendly fer a start. How am I supposed to pertect you, like that? Ain't it occurred to you, if friend Serrano's so desperate for your body he might decide to take you by force?'

'He wouldn't dare.'

'Wouldn't he?'

'Rose, Jim's got a point. We ought to put him in the spare room. So he can be close at hand.'

'Don't worry, lady. Your honour'll be safe with me. I ain't no rich Mex rancher. You ain't interested in me. And I ain't likely to be sneakin' in your room.'

The girl's pale cheeks flushed hotly. 'How dare you. Are you suggesting — ?'

'I ain't suggestin' nuthin'. It ain't none of my business why you should wanta git hitched to a man like Serrano. Or what you got up to when you *was* his fiancée. Or, perhaps it *is*. Maybe I oughta know all the facts? You ain't holdin' somethang back I oughta know?'

'Just shut up,' she snapped. 'I made a mistake. A man like you wouldn't understand. OK, you can stay in the spare room, but first you get those stinking clothes off, and take a bath.'

'Cain't smell nuthin'.' Slaughter picked his shirt up in two fingers and took a sniff. 'I thought you were short of water.'

'We've got enough for that.' Rose stood up to return to the kitchen. 'You stink like a warthog. And you've got the manners to suit. If you're to stay in this house I'd like you to behave in as civilized a manner as you can.'

'Civilized,' Slaughter muttered, as she went out. 'Thass somethang I ain't. Feisty filly, ain't she, Ben? You got a thoroughbred there, boy.'

3

James Slaughter, his hat tipped over his eyes, was snoring heavily in sleep, sprawled out on the cushioned rocker chair.

Rose, who had finished her chores in the kitchen, and locked up the henhouse for the night, returned and wrinkled her nose when she saw him. 'Is this what we have to put up with?'

'Let him sleep off the whiskey. He had a skinful,' Ben said, shaking his head, thoughtfully. 'You know, he's not as bad a man as you think. Under that leathery hide there's a spark of decency. And I think he likes you.'

'Likes me?' she exclaimed. 'Ben, I have no wish to be liked by a man like him, thank you. A drunkard, a cold-hearted mercenary, a killer. And, anyway, how do we know he is any good? He seems just like a clumsy braggart to me.'

'I have a feeling he can help us, Rose.'

Slaughter stirred under his hat, and opened one eye like a basking alligator. 'What the hell time is it?' he gasped.

Rose looked startled, wondering if he had heard her words. But she didn't care if he had. It was true.

'About ten. There's a half-moon rising.'

'Why dincha wake me?'

'You looked so sweet and innocent we didn't like to.'

'So now we've got three comedians.'

He hauled himself up and fished a cheroot stub from his shirt pocket. He struck a match on his nail and lit up, breathing out the foul smoke. 'You got a spare horse I can use?'

'Anything your highness cares for. You missed supper. Shall I fry you something up? Shall I heat your bath water?'

'Sarcasm don't suit you, lady.' He

stroked back his rumpled hair. 'The bath'll have to wait. I been thinking: when they poisoned that water-hole they knew you'd have to move your cattle back down to the Rio Diablo. That's what they want you to do. It'll make it easier for them to come across and help themselves. How far's the river?'

'About ten miles.'

'Come on, *amigo*.' He jumped to his feet, jerking his hatbrim down over his forehead. 'We gotta ride.'

'I'll go get the broncs saddled,' Ben said, dashing out.

'And you' — Slaughter turned on her with a snarl — 'you got a spare revolver in the house? I'd strongly advise you to strap it on and be ready to use it. And aincha got a rifle that holds more than one slug?'

'There's my father's Winchester and his revolver. They're still in his old bedroom.'

'Get 'em.'

He was out in the yard as Ben rode

a horse and led a spare across from the stables.

Rose came out into the moonlight. 'Wait,' she called.

The gunman swung onto the horse in one fluid motion, and turned it with his knees back to see what she wanted.

'There's some cold venison and oat cakes,' she said, pressing the linen-wrapped food into his hand. 'You can eat it as you ride. We've got to keep your strength up if you're working for us.'

Slaughter touched her face with his finger. 'You oughta smile more often. It suits you.'

He put spurs to the bronc and he and Ben went at a fast lope out past the corrals, heading out in an arrow-straight line across the sage, which gleamed silvery-blue in the moonlight. The young woman felt her cheek where he had touched her and watched them go.

'Maybe Ben's right,' she breathed. 'Maybe he's not as bad as he seems.'

★ ★ ★

The Rio Diablo was a glittering snake in the night, its water low, and all along its edge a large herd of longhorns — some 2,000 head — were dotted in clusters for a mile.

'The boys have been branding them and we're thinking of moving them out on the trail to Tucson. It's early yet, but we don't want to lose any more.'

They could see the red tips of burning cigarettes as the cowboys rode their horses around them, softly crooning some ballad or other, soothing the half-wild herd. The slightest unexpected sound might spook them into a stampede.

Ben and James Slaughter rode their broncs into the moiling throng, moving gently through them, headed for the chuckwagon and the camp-fire where those men not on guard-turn were rolled in their blankets on the ground.

A chubby cook half-rose, with a shotgun in his hand, to challenge them, but recognized Ben as he got near. 'Whoo! You didn't oughta be riding up on us in the dark like that, Mr Turner. You could be mistaken for somebody else.'

'All quiet, Bob?'

'All quiet so far, suh. The boys got two hundred head branded today. We ain't seen sight of nobody.'

'You broke out the carbines? The boys keeping them handy?'

'Yes, suh. They're sleeping with 'em by their sides.'

Ben crouched down and helped himself to coffee from the big pot which was kept always on the boil. He sucked at the steamy liquid, a worried frown on his face. He tossed the grounds on the fire and handed the empty tin mug to Slaughter.

The bounty hunter filled it and knelt on his bootheels, pondering a while. Eventually he growled, 'All I can hope is we had a wasted journey.'

He had no sooner spoken than there was the sound of gunfire from further along the river-bank. He listened, alertly. It sounded like half a mile away. 'Correction — I think we got here just in time. Wake these men. Let's ride.'

Slaughter ran to swing onto his horse, and, raking its sides with his spurs, went at a gallop along the river-bank, splashing his bronc across the shallows to the other side so he could skirt the herd. Ben went racing after him, his coat tails flying in the wind.

'Is there any place we can cut 'em off?' Slaughter shouted, hauling in his bronc to let Ben catch up.

'Yes, they'll probably cut through Crucero Canyon towards Serrano's ranch. We can reach it across the side of Tower Butte.'

'Lead on, *amigo*.'

They abandoned the river and headed their horses across a waste of waist-high, wiry creosote bushes, which made it hard going. 'Durn plants, what use are they to man or beast?' Slaughter cursed.

Tower Butte rose before them, a chimney of rock silhouetted against the night sky. 'We go across this side,' Ben said, pointing the way.

The lower slopes of the great rock were a loose mixture of slate and sand and, as they were trying to climb to more solid ground, it was even harder for their mounts to make headway. Slaughter quirted his beast onwards as it struggled and floundered, urging it to make heroic leaps upward and forward until they were beneath the chimney rock face.

The horses were frothing at the bit, foam spewing their sides, breathing hard, and the hired gun relaxed his vicious treatment and let his go at a canter around the edge of the chimney, following a narrow foot path. When he and Ben reached the far side they reined in. 'They'll be coming through Crucero Canyon if they come,' Ben said. 'On the other hand they might follow the Diablo and head for border country. There's a maze of canyons that way where they could hide.'

James Slaughter stepped down and led his bronc behind a large rock. He jerked his long-barrelled Colt Lightning rifle from out of the blanket roll, and fed a .50–95 express calibre cartridge into the breech. The extra-long bullets were big enough to take out a buffalo, or blast through a man's inside. He climbed to the top of the rock and steadied it on the rim, adjusting the sights.

'If they come this way they sure gonna git a surprise,' he muttered.

Ben ran up at a crouch to spreadeagle himself beside him and peer over the rim. He had a Springfield carbine, a lighter weapon which used a .45 bullet and 55 grains of powder, with a quarter of the range and power of the Lightning.

'I done tell your sister about them single-shot popguns,' Slaughter growled. 'Time you got yourself a man's gun.'

'It's superior to most rifles in this sandy, dusty country,' Ben said. 'I'll tell you why: because the breechblock and receiver can be easily wiped clean.'

'It weren't much use to Hardass Custer and the Seventh at the Little Big Horn. Jams at the slightest whim. That's probably why him and his got 'emselves wiped out.'

'I can hit a corral post at two hundred yards, that's good enough for me.'

'Let's hope you can hit a moving man on a hoss, 'cause here they come.'

Sure enough, a wild-eyed herd of longhorns, some 200 head, were coming at a run out of Crucero Canyon, a seething mass of horn and hide, their moans mingled with the drumming of their hooves on the hard ground. Through the darkness and dust they could see several horsemen dressed *vaquero*-style in high hats and ornately decorated leathers cracking bullwhips and lariats, urging them on.

'You try for the nearer ones,' Jim Slaughter murmured, pulling the rifle butt tight into his shoulder and taking careful aim. 'I'll take out the far side. Now!'

As their shots cracked out two of the leading *renegados* were cartwheeled from their saddles.

Ben had a line of slugs ready on the rock and, ejecting his spent case, nimbly fed another into the Springfield, cocking the hammer, and squinting along the sights again. But by then Slaughter had already levered another big bullet into his Lightning and it was whistling through the air to plummet into the chest of another *vaquero*, spurting blood as it passed right through him to plummet into the side of a mustang, which kicked up its heels as it toppled into the dust, bringing another man down.

The leading longhorns leaped with fright, swinging their huge, spear-pointed horns, but kept on a tentative run. Slaughter's third bullet put the leading bull down, which he knew would slow the herd. Meanwhile, Ben's second shot had sent another rustler spinning into Eternity.

They were not going to have it all their own way. Four more *vaqueros* emerged out of the blanket of dust, revolvers in their fists, raised to fire, and chips were chiselled from the rocks about the ambushers' heads. But two more paid for their bravery and folly, and were cartwheeled from their saddles.

'One of 'em's gittin' away,' Slaughter shouted, firing at the back of a man spurting his mustang ahead from the herd, which was slowing in puzzlement at all the noise. But the poor light and the dust made him miss by a fraction. He abandoned his rifle and ran to leap on his horse. 'Cover me, Ben.'

As he watched him go, Ben reached for the more powerful rifle and deterred two other of the Mexicans from following. He was surprised by the kick of the Lightning and its accuracy, the ease with which he dislodged another *vaquero* from his saddle. The last rustler left leapt from his horse for the cover of the rocks, and Ben made sure he kept his head down.

The fleeing *charro* had disappeared into the darkness, but Slaughter charged after him, quirting his horse from side to side as he rode. He plunged his mustang down through the loose shale to the valley floor in an effort to cut him off, and glimpsed him speeding on around a bend in the valley about fifty yards ahead. He knew his own near-exhausted mount couldn't keep up this pace for long, but he spurred him on, drawing his heavy Schofield six-gun to try for a shot. The hurtling momentum of the race, however, meant that his lead whistled harmlessly past the man's head.

The rustler had reached a Y-junction and spun his mustang to face his pursuer, replying with his own revolver. Slaughter charged head-on into the hail of bullets and felt one sear his shoulder, another clip his hat. He fired the Schofield some more and the rider, with a look of alarm, set off with alacrity along a narrower canyon.

'Hell take it!' Slaughter felt an ominous click and no response from his handgun. He was out of lead. He was almost up with the fellow. He could have had him. He kicked his horse galloping on, and shoved the Schofield back in its leather. He had no lariat with him. So he tried a desperate trick. As he came up behind the fleeing man he rode his horse deliberately into the other's back legs, sending him rolling, and nearly tripping, himself, in the process.

Slaughter was tipped over the neck of his stumbling bronc, recovered his seat and hauled his mustang round by sheer strength. He jumped from the saddle ready to do battle with his fists against the man with a gun. The mustang had rolled over, but was struggling to its feet. Its owner, however, was lying supine. Slaughter grabbed hold of him by his bandanna and shook him. There was no response. He had hit his head on a rock. He was out cold. He felt for the neck pulse. He was dead.

'Waal, thass what ye git for pizenin' wells and taking a lady's property, you coyote,' Slaughter muttered.

He let him drop back, purloining his revolver. He vaulted on to the fresher mustang, catching the reins of his own horse. He rode back at a jog to the main canyon and saw the longhorns running towards him, their heads tossing, but slower and more cautiously now. He fired a shot into the air, and, when they saw him, they ploughed to a halt.

Suddenly he heard pounding hooves coming through the darkness towards him and, at first he thought it might be Ben, or one of the other boys, so held his fire. No, it was a tall-hatted *vaquero*, running hell for leather from Ben's rifle fire. He came charging through the longhorns' dust and saw the gunman too late. Slaughter had the revolver raised and made no mistake. He blasted a slug into him, point blank, toppling him from the saddle.

Ben was not far behind, and smiled when he saw James Slaughter calmly sitting a horse, a dead man at his feet, and the herd moiling about in a circle, nervously. 'It looks like they bit off more than they could chew this time,' he said.

'Yeah,' Slaughter grunted. 'Thass the only way to stop 'em. A dose of lead in the guts is the only language these monkeys understand.'

4

'Friend Serrano ain't gonna be troubling you for a few days. We musta wiped out half his force. He'll have to hire himself some more hard men.'

'You think he'll try again?'

'What I hear of him he ain't the sort to give up. You know what Spanish pride is like. Those monkeys feel honour-bound to fight to the death.'

They were ambling on fresh horses back to the ranch the following morning. Ben Turner had lost four of his own men killed by the rustlers, and another was in a bad way. They would have to send a wagon for him so he could rest up at the ranch. Fat Bob, the cook, had been left in charge of the herd with the depleted cowhands.

'The sooner we move the herd out the happier I'll be,' Ben said. 'But it's a long trail to Tooh-sohn and the railhead. We can't do it with the few men we've got left. We're gonna need to hire more hands.'

'Crazy, innit? All this killin'. Tit for tat. Where's it git ya? Ah, well,' Slaughter sighed, 'I guess it puts cash in my pocket.'

'Range war isn't something I ever wanted to get mixed up in. I had never killed a man before last night and it's not an experience I relish repeating.'

'Aw,' Slaughter grunted. 'You git used to it.'

'Well, I would rather be back in my office chair in St Louis. But, like you say, we can't just take this sitting down. Us Anglos have our pride, too.'

The tall-hat shape of the Butte rose in front of them against a clear blue, cloudless sky and beyond that the wide blue sage tableland about the ranch house. 'You know, if it weren't for all this thievin' and killin' this could be a mighty pleasant place for a man to settle down,' James Slaughter mused.

'This border country has always been

the hangout of desperadoes, the scum of the Territory, Mex, white and 'breeds. I'll never know why Dad settled here in the first place.'

'There's somethang wild and wonderful about the scenery, I guess. And if these flotsam get the message that you ain't likely to take any nonsense they won't be so likely to harass you.'

'So, it's all down to the law of the gun? Well, it's not the kind of life I want to lead, or bring my children up to, if I should have any, that is.'

'You ain't made any plans in that direction yet?' Slaughter asked, with a scoffing grin.

'Well, yes, there is a gal in St Louis waiting for me, and the sooner I get back to her the better I'll feel.'

'So, who's gonna pretect your sister when you're gone?'

'I'm afraid she'll either have to sell up and come with me; or stay and protect herself, or find herself a good man.'

'I guess there ain't many around

up to her high standards.' They had cantered into the ranch house area by now and saw Rose standing on the porch in a white blouse and long, flared red-and-black skirt, waiting for them. 'Waal, look who's here. We were just talkin' about ya.'

'Indeed?' Rose said, superciliously inspecting the dark-haired vagrant in his sweat-stained shirt and greasy leathers. 'Am I meant to be flattered, or otherwise?'

'We was just thinkin' there ain't a man in the whole territ'ry good enough for you,' Slaughter said, with his hardly perceptible smile. 'You'll have a to send away mail order fer one. But tell him he'll need a gun if you're gonna hold onto this place.'

'I don't need a man,' she snapped. 'My family's ranched here for two generations. The Apaches couldn't shift us, so I won't let a man like Jesus del Muchado Serrano do so.'

'That's fightin' talk, lady. I hope you're up to it. Do you want the good news first, or the bad?'

'Come into the house. I've some lemonade cooling. What's happened? What's that blood on your shoulder?'

'Aw, it's only a nick.' Slaughter swung down from his horse. 'First I gotta tell you you got a brother to be proud of.'

They followed her in, and gave her an account of what had occurred, and she sat trim and serious-faced as she listened. 'Four of the men killed?' She stared at her knotted hands. 'That's terrible. Did you give them a decent burial? Oh, dear God, we should never have — '

'Fought back?' Slaughter grunted. 'You had to. And you did. It's done with now and it's given Serrano somethang to chaw on. Your men knew the score. Out here on the range they have to be prepared to protect the herd sometimes. And sometimes the odds ain't good. They did their duty, stuck by you, died valiantly.'

'Serrano's lost seven of his,' Ben put

in. 'Maybe this will stop him.'

Rose stared up at him. 'Where will it all lead? Maybe I should do as you say, Ben, sell up, go live somewhere civilized where there's decent society.'

'That's what I would urge you to do, Rose.' Ben poured her a glass of lemonade from the pitcher. 'But, I think you're like Dad. You're too damn stubborn.'

Slaughter had slumped onto the best rocker with its soft cushions. 'Aincha got nuthin' stronger to put in this?'

'No.' She straightened up and eyed him. 'I don't allow alcohol on the ranch.'

'Yeah, I mighta guessed.'

'I'll wash that gun-wound before it turns septic. You had better take your shirt off. And if you're going to stay in this house it is time for that bath. I just can't stand your stench.'

'All right. I guess I gotta humour you.'

'I was expecting you back so I've had Maria heat up the boiler in the wash house. You can go in the barrel and I'll come in and attend to your shoulder. Don't worry, I won't look at you. Just keep your back turned to me.'

'I ain't worried, gal. You can look all you like.'

Slaughter stumbled out to the wash house, and, when she heard him splashing and growling some kind of song about 'the Rose of Arizoney' she went out to him.

'That's a nasty cut.' Rose examined the bloody bullet groove across the top of the shoulder of the bounty hunter and began to dab at it with disinfectant.

'Ain't as bad as the ones them other fellas got,' he muttered. 'Yee-ouugh! Careful, thass sore.'

'I'm sorry. When you've bathed I'll put some ointment on it.' Her fingers flickered across his broad shoulders which were sunburned a dark hue, or perhaps he had a touch of Indian blood in him and it was his natural colour? 'There! Is that better?'

'That sure is. A woman's touch! That's paradise, Rose.' He handed her the brush. 'Mebbe you could scrub my back?'

'Oh, very well. But I'm not your nursemaid.'

'Hey, I lost the soap. You think you could put your fingers down here and have a feel for it?'

She pursed her lips, a slight blush rising to her pale cheeks. 'No, I don't think I will.'

'Ya gotta scrub harder than that. Jest think of me like I'm a hoss.'

'The likeness isn't far off,' she said, and scrubbed a little harder. 'How long would it be since — ?'

'Aw, about six months I s'pose.'

'There! When you get out you can wrap this big towel round you. I've had Maria wash your shirt and jeans. They shouldn't take too long to dry in the sun. As for these! — she picked up his faded pink long johns, full of worn holes — 'Eugh! These are going on the fire.'

'What am I gonna wear?'

'I'll look you out an old pair of Dad's. At least they'll be clean. Oh, my God!'

With a whoosh of the water her hired gun hand stood up and faced her. For a second Rose stared in amazement at his wide chest matted with black hair which trickled down to his loins. He was built like a stallion. 'Cain't you do nuthin' fer this?' he asked, pointing a finger.

'How dare you?' Rose backed away, trying not to look. 'How foul!'

But she was back up against the wall and he was reaching out his muscled arms to grasp her shoulders and pull her into him. 'Waal, it's your fault. You done it to me. All that touchin'.'

'Get off!' She gave a scream and pushed him away. 'Don't touch me.'

Slaughter lost his balance and toppled backwards, the barrel spilling over and, hanging onto her, he rolled, crashing back onto the concrete floor. Rose screamed again as she fell on top of him, trying to save herself, ungainly, slipping on the streaming suds. He still had hold of her, pulling her face to his, trying to kiss her. She felt his tongue lick her cheek and screamed again, thrusting him away. 'You foul person. You — oh — you!'

She rolled away, sitting in the pool of water, showing her stockings, her violet eyes blazing furiously, and, yet somehow hypnotized by him. 'You're really disgusting.'

'What's the matter, lady? Ain't ya seen one afore?'

'No, I haven't,' she shouted, picking herself up with what dignity she could. At the door she tried not to glance back. 'Nor do I want to again, thank you.'

She slammed the door shut and was breathing hard as she leaned against it on the other side. 'What an awful man. What am I going to do?'

Suddenly she heard Slaughter begin laughing, out loud, honking and braying like a mule. She straightened her skirt and hurried into the house, but she could still hear him laughing. It was as if he would never stop. 'God! I hate him,' she whispered.

★ ★ ★

'What's wrong, Rose? Something upset you?'

'It's him.' She sat in the rocker clutching her elbows. 'He ... he insulted me. He's depraved. He ought to be locked up.'

'What did he do?' Gradually he coaxed it out of her, fearing the worst. But when she said that the gunman had 'exposed' himself, Ben could not help smiling. 'Well, what do you expect, if you go poking about in there when he's in the tub?'

'It's disgusting.' She thought of Jim Slaughter sprawled on the floor blatantly naked, grinning at her. 'Anywhere else a man who insulted a woman like that would be arrested, probably lynched.'

'You're a good-looking girl, Rose. You've blossomed out. Even I noticed that. It's only natural. You're bound to have men want you. And around here most men are like him, coarse and dangerous. I've told you, you shouldn't be here on your own.'

She made a grimace of her lips, solemn-faced, and squeezed sudsy water from her skirt. 'Perhaps you're right.'

'You deserve a better life. Back East you could mingle in decent society, meet a better class of man, a man of substance, a gentleman, someone who would treat you like a lady. I don't like leaving you here.'

'He is dangerous,' she hissed, glancing back at the wash-house. 'He's only been here a day and he's already turned you into a killer. He wants me to strap on Dad's revolver. There are nearly a dozen men dead. Death follows him. He is one of the damned, you can tell that. He cares for nobody. He wants to drag us into damnation with him.'

'Isn't that rather overstating the case? But I'm inclined to agree. I don't want any more killing. We could sell up. Offer the stock and land to Serrano half price. What are the beeves worth in Kansas, fifteen dollars? Let him have them for seven a head. To tell the truth, all this land, it's not worth a lot, not with him as a neighbour. Nobody else is going to want to buy.'

Rose was deep in thought for moments, and started as she heard the wash-house door open. 'Get rid of him,' she snapped. 'Pay him off. Sell up.'

James Slaughter sauntered in, a towel around his waist, found a match and lit a stub of cigar. He hooked a leg over a chair and leaned on its back. His green eyes glimmered in their craggy slots, his face immobile. 'What's goin' on?'

'We've had enough of bloodshed. We're getting out.'

'What's happened to the ole frontier spirit?' He trickled out smoke from his lips. 'This mornin' it was, 'The 'pache never beat us, no damn Mex will'.'

'You sicken us, Mr Slaughter,' Rose said. 'You were aptly named. Take your money and go.'

Ben had opened the safe, and was counting out $500. 'When you came here, I asked you to respect my sister. I would have thought an apology was in order.'

The bounty hunter accepted the cash, in his cigar hand, and spread his left hand wide. 'Come on.' He grinned widely at Rose. 'I only wanted yuh to shake hands with my best friend. Cain't you take a joke?'

'That was not my idea of a joke.' Rose's face was severe as she glanced at the half-naked man with his muscular, sculpted shoulders, and quickly averted her eyes. 'If I ever lie with a man it will be when I am honourably married in the sight of God for the purpose of procreating children.'

'Yek! Yek! Yek! What kinda mealy-mouthed virgin we got here?'

'That's enough, Jim. You can take

a siesta along in your room 'til your clothes dry. Then we'd like you to go.'

'I understand there are a couple of unfortunate hussies who cater to the lusts of men like you along at the saloon in San Andreas,' Rose said. 'I suggest you go visit them.'

'They ain't my type.' He rose from his chair, picked up his revolver and ammunition belt and started to leave the room. 'I prefer a feisty gal, like you.'

'Can't you get it in your thick head?' she hissed. 'I'm not interested in a drifter, a professional killer. Just go. Leave us alone.'

'Maybe I'll go see Jesus Serrano. I ain't finished yet.' He turned on his bare heel, ignoring the cash, and jabbed his cigar stub at her. 'I said until completion. Lady, I ain't even started yet.'

5

It was a strange sensation to be naked and clean between the sheets of a bed in the shady room. He was used to sleeping under the stars on hard earth, always half-alert for prowlers in the night. He stuffed the Schofield under the soft pillow, but when he closed his eyes his mind became filled with images of the young woman. He twisted and turned, restlessly, but gradually drifted off. In his dream she was still with him, swimming naked in a deep pool, inviting him in. He knew it would be freezing cold, but he slid off a cliff top, fully-dressed, gun and boots, plunging down into the water. She was screaming, struggling, pushing him away, and they were going down, down, down . . .

Slaughter woke, as if bursting to the surface, but she was nowhere around.

The house seemed deserted. By the sun's shadow on the wall he guessed it was about four. He saw that someone had tossed a pair of long drawers down on his bed. And the pile of money on the bedside table. 'Wimmin,' he muttered, as he swung out and pulled the drawers on. 'They're more trouble than they're worth. All that fussin'.' He wondered about the dream. It did not portend good. Still, it was better than those other nightmares, the images of the war, the faces of the men he had killed. Eugh!

He stared at the cash, shrugged and scooped it up. He wandered out to the back yard and found his sun-dried jeans and shirt. His thick woollen socks had been washed, too, and a hole darned. On the line were also pegged boiled strips of the longhorn he had shot, which had been slaughtered for its meat. It was being dried as beef jerky. He took a couple of hunks and wrapped it in newspaper. He pulled on his boots, shotgun chaps, buckled his gunbelt, picked up his Navajo poncho, and went to saddle his pinto in the stable. He filled his wooden water canteen at the well, took a sup of the cool liquid, himself, and looked across at the wagon shed. He could hear Rose talking to the old farrier. Ben had disappeared. They were obviously keeping out of his way.

Slaughter rolled the Lightning in his blanket and tied it behind the saddle. He swung aboard and, jerking his hat down to shade his eyes, headed out at a fast clip towards the westering sun. He could see far off, beyond the Rio Diablo, the jagged tooth ridge of the Diablo mountains in their heat haze, the terrain of the man he intended to meet.

Rose came from the wagon shed and watched him go, riding broad-shouldered, straight-backed, determined. 'Thank goodness he's gone,' she whispered. And then a thought struck her. He wouldn't be so low as to offer his services to Jesus Serrano, would he?

★ ★ ★

It was dusk by the time the bounty hunter reached the cattle camp on the Diablo river, if river it could be called, for most of it had by now evaporated in the summer drought and only a shallow stream still trickled. 'Howdy,' he called to Fat Bob who was dishing out thick beef stew to the boys. 'Looks like I'm just in time for supper.'

When he had filled his belly, supped hot coffee and smoked a while, he mounted his bronc and headed across the river into enemy country. Tower Butte rose, a 300 foot tall sentinel in the night. He manoeuvred around its scrubby base and reached the spot of the gunfight. Several of the *vaqueros* were sprawled in postures of death, as they had fallen, minus their guns and boots, which the Arizona cowboys had looted. The ants, coyotes and vultures had already made a start on their bodies, and the ribs of the dead mustang were almost picked clean, perhaps by a mountain lion.

'Critters got to eat,' he muttered, and headed on into the unknown.

Three hours of careful riding through the half-darkness as the silver globe of moon rose brought him to a ridge from which he could look down upon the *estancia* of Jesus del Muchado Serrano. In the centre of a rocky basin stood a colonial-style ranch house glimmering stucca-white in the moonlight, its pillared portico rising to an ornately domed roof, somewhat like a church. Perhaps it had been one of the Franciscan missions built by the men who followed in the footsteps of the *conquistadors* and tried to tame the Indians' souls. The Apache had been fighting them for nigh on 400 years.

Slaughter saw a movement on the parapet, the glint of moonlight on the weapon of a guard. And the glimmer of the red points of the *cigarillos* of men on horseback patrolling the adobe wall that surrounded the fortress.

'A man sure ain't gonna git in there

without being spotted.' Slaughter let his pinto nibble at what nourishment he could find among the thorns, pulled his waterproof Navajo *serape* over his head against the night cold and settled down to wait.

The valley was the usual lunar landscape of sand, rock and shale, scattered with mesquite, sage brush, yucca, Spanish bayonet, and great rocks standing as if tossed down haphazardly by some giant hand. How the huge herds of longhorns managed to proliferate on hostile land like that was a mystery. But where the coyote could survive, so could longhorns, and so could man.

'There's no wonder Serrano covets Rose's land,' Slaughter growled. 'She's got a nice long stretch of grama grass her side of the river. She'd be a fool to give it up.' The pinto spluttered his lips at him by way of reply. 'Hell, I gotta quit talkin' to this dumb hoss.'

He propped himself against a rock and catnapped, waking at the slightest sound or movement. But it would only be one of the small animals, the kit-foxes, the kangaroo rats, the mice and snakes that lay under their rocks all day to avoid the 120 degree heat and came out hunting at night. Maybe even a gila monster, the four-foot long meat-eating lizard. Or, maybe a black panther. Both were still not extinct in spite of man's guns and poisons. The screech of an owl woke him before dawn and he opened his eyes to see it glide, white and ghostly to swoop on its startled prey. Kill or be killed, that was the law of the desert.

When the sun's effulgent rays began to radiate across the landscape, flushing the cliffs and rocks red, announcing another scorching day, Slaughter made a move. He tightened the cinch of the saddle and a notch of his gunbelt and, as a second thought, tucked his $1,000 beneath a rock, taking note of the spot, an oddly shaped agave hanging over it. He climbed on his bronc and rode down into the valley heading in as straight a line as possible towards the *Tejon Rancho.*

When he neared the house a shot cracked out, the bullet whanging close, chipping rocks, and ricocheting away. He raised a gloved hand in a peace sign. The second slug nearly took off his fingers and the pinto leaped with alarm, whinnying his terror. Slaughter barely flinched, holding the wild-eyed horse in a hard grip and spurring him on.

'Bastards,' he growled. 'They can see I'm alone.'

Suddenly a pack of *vaqueros* were racing towards him across the half-mile distance, surrounding him, shrieking and yelling in their shrill language, grinning like white-fanged wild dogs as they covered him with the deathly holes of their revolvers. '*Vamos, gringo,*' one shouted, prodding him with a rifle.

'*Señor* Serrano, is he at home?' the *Americano* asked. 'I wanna talk to him.'

'Oh, he ees home,' a man said.

'Don't worry. We take you.'

At that, they charged off towards the shimmering white-washed building, Slaughter put to a gallop among them.

'Look what we catch, *señor*,' the man called Raoul, who could speak English, cried, as a man stepped out onto the veranda. 'A lousy steenking *greengo*.'

The man was about thirty, the tight curls of his head already becoming grizzled with grey. His bronzed face was not unhandsome, but there was a cruel gleam to his muddy eyes. His loose white shirt was ruched at the front and cuffs, fallen apart to reveal his bronzed bare chest, and he wore tight velveteen trousers, richly embroidered with gold, above silver-toed boots.

'I guess you must be Jesus Serrano,' Slaughter said, still on horseback, as the men milled about him.

'You guess right, *hombre*. Don't you know that *Americanos* are not welcome here? What are you doing on my land?

We have a war on.'

'Yuh. So I heard. That's what brings me here.'

'Who are you? What you want?' Serrano had a seven-shot Spencer carbine in his hands, and he thumbed the hammer, ominously. 'You better talk fast, *Yanqui*.'

'Let's say I'm a soldier of fortune. And I ain't a Yankee. I fought for the South in the War of Rebellion. But that's all water under the bridge. These days I'm usually a bounty hunter. You know what that is?'

'Sure, I know what that is. But why come here' — Serrano smiled, flashing white teeth, as his men laughed — 'there's no bounty on my head? I might have killed a few men but they asked for it.'

'Yuh, they usually do.' Slaughter stroked his grey jaw and his face was expressionless as the rider with the rifle got close and poked him again. He flicked him away as if he might be an irritating fly. 'I was in San Andreas deliverin' the corpse of a bad boy called Jed Hanks. Business was slack in the Fargo office, but in the saloon they said you was havin' some kinda war. So I figured you might like to hire my gun.'

'You don' say? An' who tol' you this?'

'The barkeep. Who else?'

'You wouldn't happen to know a woman called Rose Turner? Or her brother, Ben Turner?'

'Nope. But I ran into some boys along the Diablo last night who said they worked for 'em. Like you, they were kinda suspicious.'

'Why come to me, *Yanqui*? Why not work for the Turners? They're more your kind.'

'I ain't got no kind. OK, to tell the truth I bumped into Turner in town. But I don't go a ball on them fancy-talkin' dudes. I offered him my services but he wouldn't pay my price. He turned me down. So, I figured I'd try you. It don't matter to me whose side I fight for as long as I git paid.'

'Oh, yes?' Serrano smiled, dubiously. 'And what is your price?'

'I guess we better discuss that in private.'

Serrano gave a wry grimace, and shrugged. 'OK, Raoul and his boys will show you in. I have to go talk to my foreman. I will be with you in a few moments.'

Slaughter looked about him, and stepped down, with his customary easy-flowing motion, the muscular grace of some panther on the prowl. 'Maybe they could give my bronc some water while we're inside? We come a long way.'

'Of course, *amigo*. Anything you say.' Serrano grinned, sardonically, and stuck out his hand. 'And perhaps you could hand over that revolver? Just a precaution, you understand?'

'Sure.' Slaughter eased the Schofield from its holster and handed it, butt forward, to the Mexican. As Raoul jabbed him in the back once more, prodding him towards the house, he growled, 'Mebbe you could tell this clown to quit jabbing me? It ain't hospitable.'

'Of course.' Serrano reeled out some Spanish, his men cackled some more, and Slaughter was jabbed forwards up the steps to the veranda and into the cool shade of the house. 'Welcome to my *casa*,' Serrano shouted after him.

When the American had disappeared into the depths of the mansion, Serrano pulled his Colt Lightning rifle free of the blanket roll behind the pinto. He levered a brass-jacketed slug into the breech and removed it with his fingers. He studied the long, snub-nosed manstopper and gave a low whistle. 'So this is where those I found in my men came from?'

Slaughter was shown, or prodded, into a high, domed banqueting hall with a huge fireplace of red rock, empty now, simply furnished with a long dining-table, a massive chair of horn and hide at its head. The whitewashed walls were hung with an assortment of Indian trophies, shields, spears, scalps, bows, medicine drums, and even what appeared to be a shrunken human head. A timbered gallery half-way up the hall revealed doors leading to other rooms. Further off in the stone-flagged house he could hear the clatter of cooking sounds as if breakfast was being prepared in the kitchens.

'So, you say you fought with the Southern Army in their misguided war,' Serrano said, as he joined them, and slumped into the horn chair. 'Who were you with?'

'Nathan Forrest. One of the finest guerilla leaders known to man. We operated in Kentucky-Tennessee, mostly behind enemy lines, blowing bridges, wrecking trains, attacking gunboats on the river, destroying their lines of communications. Since then I've used my skills as a lone operator.'

'What is your name? Your rank?'

'Lt Colonel James Slaughter, only I don't use the fancy title no more.

Promotion comes easy in a war.'

'Forrest? Didn't he make his fortune from slaves?'

'Thass right. And he spent it on arming his regiment.'

'And you think he was a great man?'

'The greatest. He didn't have no West Point training, but he could have shown Napoleon Bonaparte a trick or two.'

'You don't say? And you believe some of those tricks may be of use to me?'

'Mebbe.' Slaughter was standing before the seated man and couldn't help having the feeling he was being interrogated. 'War teaches a man a few ways to survive.'

'Tell me; I am interested in war, Colonel Slaughter. What makes you think this General Forrest was so brilliant?'

'Aw, I could talk about it all night. Let's just say if President Jeff Davis had listened to him, put him in command of our western sector, we needn't have surrendered. We couldn't have won, no way, but we coulda held 'em to a draw. The Yankees would have had to recognize our rights to secession. Thangs woulda taken a different turn, believe me.'

'Believe you?' Serrano was jogging the manstopper bullet up and down in his hand. 'What position did you hold?'

'Commander of one of General Forrest's brigades of cavalry.'

'That's odd. It may surprise you, but I have studied your Civil War. I have read of this Forrest, his commanders, Colonel Rucker, General Buford, Captain Boone, Brigadier Bell, Captain Jackson ... but I don't remember any mention of a Colonel Slaughter.'

Slaughter had noticed the manstopper and his expression, if that were possible, froze into even more of a rutted stoneface. 'What you gittin' at?'

'I am saying you are a liar.' He held up the manstopper between thumb and finger. 'You are a lousy *gringo* liar come to spy on me.'

The bounty hunter braced himself, as if to spring forward, but the man with the rifle nudged him and growled, 'You move iss last theeng you do.'

Serrano smiled at him. 'You killed at least four of my men the night before last. Shot them from their saddles. These bullets, they tear a man or horse to pieces. Not very pleasant. I have never seen one before. Isn't there some talk of them being banned?'

'Mebbe there is. How should I know?'

Serrano rapped the bullet on the table and a hugely corpulent serving woman shuffled in. 'Where is breakfast? I am hungry. Don't worry about the *gringo*. Bring it in, Maria.'

He shouted out in Spanish and three more of his men came into the room, carbines in their hands. 'You are not only a liar, you are a murderer and a thorn in my flesh. Give me one reason why I should not kill you.'

Before he could move, a tall *vaquero* with a thin, cruel-cut face stepped forward and hammered the butt of his carbine across Slaughter's jaw, Another man moved in to double him up with a jab of his carbine into his gut. While the third kicked him a stinging blow behind the knees, knocking him to the floor. As he tried to regain his feet they began kicking and pummelling him.

'Come on, woman,' Serrano roared, beckoning the servant forward. 'What are you hanging about for? Come round this side. Ah, very nice,' he sighed, as he uncovered a silver salver on the tray. '*Heuvos rancheros*. Just what I fancy.'

He began stuffing his mouth with dripping eggs in oil and sour cream, with red hot peppers, as his men punched and thumped the American around the room. Slaughter roared like a rutting bull and managed to swing several haymakers, knocking one of the *vaqueros*, tumbling into the fireplace, but they were impossible odds and he was down on his knees again, grunting as the blows hit him.

'OK, OK.' Serrano raised a hand. 'Don't kill him just yet. How's he doing?'

Slaughter half-raised himself, his black hair hanging over his face, and wiped blood from his nose. 'OK. So, I was working for Rose Turner. But I ain't now, OK. Man can change sides, cain't he?'

'Why this sudden change of heart, *gringo*?'

' 'Cause I tried to git fresh with her. She didn't like it. Fired me.'

'Fresh? What is this?'

'I tried it on,' he shrugged, feeling his jaw. 'Tried to rape the bitch, no doubt like you did.'

'Like I did? What you talking about?'

'She broke off your engagement, didn't she? She's a mighty sassy lady.'

'*Si*, she is. But what happened between us is nothing to do with you. Sure, I hate her. She *is* a bitch. And I am going to break her.'

'Come off it. I can read between the

lines. You wanted her. You wanted her land and dowry. But you couldn't wait to have her body. You tried to rape her, and I bet she either kicked you in the *cojones* — '

Serrano gave a roar of laughter, and poured himself coffee. '*Si*! The bitch smashed a chair across my head. When I came to she was gone. She rode out of here. She is a crazy woman. She owes me.'

The Mexican got to his feet, wiped the egg from his mouth on a cloth, and drawled, 'You know, I like you. I like your nerve. But I owe *you*, too.' He kicked his spurred heel into Slaughter's face and the American fell back, spitting blood and cursing.

'You lousy cowards,' Slaughter grunted. 'Do your worst.'

'Cowards?' Serrano kicked him again. 'So you want me to let the boys have fun with you, eh? We will see who is the coward. Why you really come here?'

He snapped out orders and the men hauled Slaughter up, dragged him out to the veranda and pitched him into the dust. 'The boys like to play the chicken run,' he laughed, as Slaughter staggered to his feet.

A lariat noose came spinning through the air to drop over the American's shoulders and, before he could hardly get hold of it, it was wound tight over the saddle horn of one of the *vaqueros*, who pricked in his heels to send his mustang galloping away.

Jesus Serrano stood for a few minutes watching the gunman being dragged through the dust, back and forth, trying to keep a grip on the rawhide rope, as the men chased after him, whooping and screaming like Apaches, cracking their whips across his back, shredding his shirt.

The rancher went back inside, resumed his seat at the table, and finished scooping up his breakfast. He pondered over a cup of coffee and murmured, 'That Turner woman. It's time I taught her a lesson, a lesson she won't forget.'

6

Jesus del Muchado Serrano rode his white stallion at a high-stepping trot into the dusty main street of San Andreas, sunlight glinting on the silver of his bridle and saddle horn, on the silver toes of his ornately tooled black boots. The wide brim of his sombrero was also weighted with silver conchos, and, all in all, the magnificent horse and his outfit proclaimed his wealth, his power.

By contrast, the few homesteaders and citizens, who paused to watch Serrano and his men ride by, were a shabby bunch. The men were in grimy work clothes, battered hats, bandannas around their necks to protect against the haze of red dust kicked up by the horse traffic. The women were in figure-muffling dresses billowing to their toes, poke bonnets supposedly protecting their weatherbeaten features from the blazing sun. They looked up with a kind of awe and fear at the gun-laden riders passing by. It was as if the *conquistadors* still owned this land.

In fact, thirty years had passed since this land had ceased to be an outpost of the Mexican empire. When American troops rode into Mexico City there had been an abject surrender and Arizona, California, and other vast tracts had been ceded to the US government. But the way of life had changed little for the former Mexican population. The army had laid seige to the Apache in their mountain strongholds. White settlers and miners had arrived to establish small communities in the harsh frontier lands. Eventually, the Apache defeated and deported to the dungeons of Florida, the railroad had reached Tucson, and with it carpet-baggers, sharpjack lawyers, businessmen building hotels and gambling hells, land-grabbers, and the usual contingent of desperadoes looking for the main-chance or on the lam.

San Andreas, isolated among the rugged hills of the border, was a little outpost of America, with its clapboard houses, white-painted fences, and even a few flower-beds planted with marigolds. It had a steepled church, a saloon, hotel, livery, a dance hall and assembly rooms, and a few houses for the men who worked in the nearby copper mines. But, mostly, the Anglos kept to themselves. And the Latinos went on with their lives in the timeless manner they had done for centuries. They scratched livings of sorts from the harsh country, looking forward to their next fiesta or saint's day. Most were desperately poor. And a few, like Serrano, extremely rich, and, with their guns, capable of flouting with impunity white men's laws.

'What can I do about it?' the overweight guardian of law, Moses Murdoch, protested when Rose Turner burst into his office demanding to know what steps he had taken to arrest the men who had poisoned her water.

'You know who it is. Jesus Serrano is the only one who could be behind it. And he is here in town today.'

'Yeah, I seen him ride in.' Moses wiped a trickle of sweat from his temple and shifted uncomfortably behind his desk. 'What can I do aginst him and a dozen armed men?'

'He is responsible for the rustling of my stock and the deaths of four of my men. We recognized the attackers. For God's sake, we killed seven of them, in self-defence, I might add, to protect and retrieve our herd. We are willing and ready to swear out warrants against Serrano, to give evidence in court.'

'Evidence. What evidence, Miss Turner? You ain't got no hard evidence far as I can see. These disputes between neighbours, they ain't easy to settle. There's two sides the question. Looks to me like he's lost more than you.'

'What did I tell you.' Ben Turner sighed. 'You're not going to get any action out of this barrel of lard. All he ever does is sit on his backside.'

'Now that, ain't fair, Mr Turner. In fact, that's libel, that is.'

'You mean slander? But how can it be, if it's true?'

'How much is Serrano paying you?' Rose demanded.

'That's another libel, or slander, whatever.' Murdoch pointed a finger at her. 'You wanta watch out, throwing accusations like that around. It's you could end up in court.'

'Oh, well, it hardly matters now,' Rose said. 'You may have the satisfaction of knowing that I am selling up. I have decided to join my brother in more civilized parts.'

'You are?' Moses looked up, his eyes bulging like a fat frog's. 'That *is* news. I heard you and Señor Serrano had agreed a meet. But I didn't know what fer. Waal, I think you're doing the right thing, Miss Rose. Ranchin' ain't wimmin's work.'

'Yes, no doubt you would think so.

It's Señor Serrano, is it, now?' Ben asked, sarcastically. 'You seem to have an uncommon respect for that man.'

'I treat all sides with respect, sir. I don't have no prejudice aginst the greasers.'

'Sure, respect for Serrano's silver, and his guns. Come on, Rose. I find the smell in here rather offensive.'

They left Moses Murdoch's adobe office and jail-house and stepped out into the harsh glare of morning sunlight. Across the way, outside Lawyer Skinner's office were several *vaqueros*, a couple still on horseback, their carbines and revolvers much in evidence, others sat on the sidewalk, or leaned in the shade of the canopy against the wall.

Rose had sent a message by the mail rider proposing this meeting, but her throat tightened at the sight of the *viciosos*, at the prospect of meeting Jesus Serrano once more.

When he first came courting her, the handsome and aristocratic Mexican had seemed to possess the qualities of a possible marriage partner, if partner she had to have. His old-world manners, his handsome, flashing-toothed charm, his breeding, all appealed to her. And, she had to admit, his possession of a large tract of land and the fine mansion on the other side of the Rio Diablo would ideally complement her own land. How he had come by them she was not sure. He seemed to have appeared out of nowhere. She had been young, just seventeen, and he had somewhat swept her off her feet. To marry and unite their fortunes seemed a sensible and romantic arrangement. In some ways Serrano was admirable, educated, fluent in Spanish and English, with an interest in learned subjects, admittedly manly ones like armaments, war, and horse bloodstocks, but no dummy. He oozed charm, and she had been taken in. That was, until she discovered his darker side.

'He must have gone in,' Ben said. 'At least, he's on time.' He took her arm and led her through the waiting men. One of them, leaned languidly against the wall smoking a cigarette, said something in Spanish that made the others laugh. Something crude, no doubt. They ignored them and went inside.

'*Buenas*, Roseta.' There was a thorny gleam in Serrano's dark eyes as he met her violet ones, a gleam, perhaps, of hatred, still mingled with love and avarice. 'We meet again. It has been a long time.'

'Almost a year,' she replied. 'A year in which my father died and you have given me nothing but trouble.'

'Me?' He touched his chest with an air of amused innocence. 'I told you before, Roseta, you have got me all wrong. Why do you bear me this grudge?'

'It is you who has borne *me* the grudge. But I am here to tell you you have won. I am ready to sell.'

Lawyer Skinner, as razor-thin as his name implied, had swung round in his swivel chair, rising, indicating chairs.

'That's what we're here to discuss. Maybe you two should keep personal feelin's outa this.'

'By all means,' Rose said. 'You have a copy of the deeds to the ranch, Mr Skinner, and my detailed assessment of the property. I am willing to accept exactly half of my estimated worth.'

'You have an independent valuer's report which accords with our figures,' Ben put in. 'My sister is only cutting her price because of the pressure put on her by this man. She has had enough, she wants out, a quick sale.'

'Hold on,' Serrano smiled. 'These are harsh words. Miss Turner is not the only one to have been plagued by rustlers. I object to you pointing the finger at me. I, too, have had my losses, my stock stolen by *bandidos*. They operate across the border. You know this country is rife with them.'

'No doubt you've had your water poisoned, too?'

'Gentlemen, this is not a law court. Let's just keep to the question in hand.

Unless, of course, you're interested in litigation against each other? Those are mighty imflammable remarks, Mr Turner.'

'OK. Get on with it. Being next to this fellow makes me want to puke.'

The dark, oak-hard face of Serrano tensed, but he tossed off the insult with a grin, and picked up the valuation report to study it. 'Hm,' he muttered, gutturally, 'I wouldn't agree with this. Some of these figures are highly fanciful.'

'Take it or leave it,' Rose said. 'I won't take a cent below.'

'I wonder — ' Serrano tossed the papers back on the desk. 'I wonder if Señorita Turner and I might have a word in private?'

Rose shook her head, alarmed, but Skinner looked at his watch and said, 'As buyer and vendor, prospective, that is, I don't see why not. If you're agreed, miss? Me and your brother'll step outside for a smoke.'

'I see no reason for this,' Rose

protested. 'Oh, very well. Give us five minutes at the most.'

When the door had closed behind them, her face hardened and she said, 'Well, Jesus, what do you want?'

'I want an end to this foolishness, Roseta.' Serrano's voice was gruff as he stared at her, as if he had difficulty in controlling his emotion. 'I have no wish to cheat you of your land. I don't want you to go. We could still be partners.'

'No, that's out of the question. Not after the things you have done. I don't trust you.'

'I admit I was angry, I was jealous, I was upset, I did some foolish things. I am a man, Roseta, I got carried away on the heat of passion. That water poisoning: it was Raoul. He acted out of misguided loyalty to me, malice to you. It was not my order, I swear.'

'It makes no difference now.'

Suddenly Jesus was down on one knee, his strong, bronzed hand gripping hers. 'Forgive me, Roseta. It was my love for you made me mad. To see you again, it is so good, like bathing in a cooling stream. Let us be friends, let us be lovers again. You once promised to marry me. Won't you renew your vow, Roseta? Marry me.'

'We were never lovers!' She tried to shake free her hand, disturbed by his closeness, his falsely adoring eyes, tried to rise to her feet. 'No! You know why I broke it off. You hit me.'

It returned to her, his pleading like this a year before. They were at his *casa*. They had kissed. She had allowed him some familiarities. But suddenly his horny hand had slapped viciously across her face. It was as if he had gone mad, he was trying to pull her clothes off, tear them from her body, dragging her into a bedroom. She had kneed him where she knew it hurt. And as, for moments, he grovelled in pain, she had picked up a heavy dining-chair, smashed it across his back. He had fallen unconscious. She had fled from the mansion, under the eyes of the startled guards, sobbing, climbing onto her horse, riding like the wind until she reached the Rio Diablo, until she was home.

'Oh, that!' he grinned, standing and putting his arms around her waist, pressing her back over Skinner's desk. 'That was only a lover's tiff. I forgive you, Roseta, as you should forgive me.'

'Leave me be,' she gasped, for his hard, male body was thrusting itself into her, and his fingers were caressing her cheek as he stared into her eyes. 'If this is all you've got to say. You thief, you murderer! Get off me!'

'Come on, Roseta. You know you still have feelings for me,' he whispered. He was careful, this time, not to allow her knee between his legs, and, indeed, had his strong horseman's thighs insinuated between hers, giving her little doubt of what he wanted from her. 'Be gentle to me, Roseta.' His lips were close to hers, as, struggling, she turned her face away from his kisses.

'Be kind to me. You know I love you. You know you love me.'

It was all happening over again! His unwanted over-perfumed, but masculine-smelling strength, his falsely persuasive caresses ... he made her skin crawl. He would not desist. In her panic her fingers were reaching out over the desk top as she was forced backwards. They came in contact with Skinner's lead paperweight. She cracked it across Serrano's temple and he fell back. 'There!' she breathed.

He was down on one knee again, holding fingers to a trickle of blood, his face contorted with pain and fury. 'You hell-cat!'

'This meeting's over.' She was rearranging her clothing, backing away to the door, still holding the paperweight. 'You can't play the same trick twice.'

'You fool! Why are you wearing that shabby peasant skirt? You are beautiful, Roseta. You deserve more. I could give you satins and silks, silver, jewellery, a fine house, servants to wait on you, land, possessions, children, we could have everything. You deserve it, Roseta. You want it. You have Mexican blood in you, too. You know that.'

His words stopped her in her her tracks. He was getting to his feet, smiling again, his dark eyes mocking her, but wary this time. 'Whoo!' he said. 'You can give a man quite a crack. I like fire in a woman, Roseta. I mean what I say. Marry me.'

'I'm leaving, Jesus. You must be mad to think I could ever want you. Are you paying the price I ask for my ranch, or not?'

'You bitch,' he snarled, pointing a finger at her. 'I'll get your ranch. But I won't pay your price.'

'In that case we have nothing more to say.' She had composed herself, stroking back the thick waves of black hair that had tumbled across her face in the struggle. 'I will call the others in.'

'By the way, I have your man,' he

growled, as she turned to the door. 'Your hired killer. What's he call himself, Lieutenant Colonel Slaughter?'

'What?' she said, sharply. 'What are you talking about, lieutenant colonel?'

'He tried to pretend he was some kind of war hero. But he won't be much of a hero by the time my men have finished with him. They will cut off his *cojones*.'

'What? You wouldn't?'

'Make him less than a man? I have left him at the *rancho* with Raoul. He is very handy with a knife is Raoul. And he has a very cruel sense of humour. Does that upset you? I see it seems to.'

Rose bit hard to repress the tremble of her lip. 'It doesn't upset me. I don't give a damn about him. Nor him about me. I thought he had gone to offer to fight for you.'

'He did, but I am not sure that I trust him. You know the old saying, if in doubt, cut him out.'

'He's just a hired killer. What have

you got against him? I would have thought you two would have got on famously.'

'Ha! So you *are* pleading his case? There's something between you?'

'Don't be so stupid. I only knew the thug one day and sent him packing. He is just the sort to serve you. Anyway, do as you wish. This conversation is over.' Rose opened the door and called out. 'Will you come in, Mr Skinner? Ben?'

'So, how did you get on?' Skinner asked brightly, but seeing Serrano dabbing his temple, added, 'Oh, not so well.'

'The negotiations were negative. You can return those documents to your safe.'

'Aren't you gonna make any offer, Señor Serrano?'

'I've made my offer to the lady. She turned me down. So, as far as the land's concerned ... what's it worth?' Serrano snapped his fingers. 'Two hundred dollars. That's what I bid.'

'That's derisory,' Ben cried. 'You're joking.'

'No joke,' Serrano smiled. 'Why don't you put it up for auction? See what you get.'

Rose eyed him, her face tense. 'Come on, Ben. You're wasting your breath.' She paused and forced a bitter smile. 'Talking about that, I always meant to tell you, Jesus, you have terrible bad breath. Quite foul. You ought to do something about it. You won't get a wife that way.'

Ben chuckled as they eased their way out through Serrano's men. 'Ouch! My li'l sister's still got claws.'

7

'Life sure is a bitch.' Slaughter groaned in agony as he tried to move. He lay on the floor of the gloomy bare cell and contemplated his unpromising future. 'Why did I come pokin' my nose in here?'

When he had breakfasted, Jesus Serrano had taken a seat on his veranda and watched his men drag Slaughter around in the dust, their bullwhips cracking like pistol shots. When he had tired of the sport, and the American lay before him, torn and bloody from the knocks and lashes, he had smiled and asked, 'Enjoy the ride, *amigo*?'

Slaughter remembered peering through his half-closed, fist-swollen eyes, through the haze of his half-consciousness, and seeing the devilishly grinning man, hearing him shout, 'Throw him in the hole.'

So, it could be worse! They hadn't killed him. Yet! And, if he knew these men, they had plenty more excruciating tortures they could practise on him. The Spanish had taught even the *Apache* a thing or two in that line. He wondered, gloomily, what else they had in mind. He had lain all day and night, hardly able to move. Apart from the random cuts and whip-openings of his flesh, it felt like his ribs had been stoved in. The small finger of his left hand was broken. And one ankle didn't feel too good. He had to support himself against the wall if he tried to rise. But, at the moment, all he wanted to do was lie there on the floor.

The next morning — indicated only by the glimmer of light that penetrated this cellar area — he had heard men's voices and the jangle of spurs as they descended steps and approached. The door of his cell was unlocked and he saw Serrano again, the man they called Raoul standing behind him.

'So, *hombre*, how you feel now?'

Serrano had grinned. 'I am summoned to go into town to meet with the beautiful Roseta Turner. You remember her, your former boss? I believe she has decided to surrender to my charm. She sees it is pointless fighting me. I will leave you in the capable hands of Raoul.'

Slaughter looked up at him and growled through puffed-up lips, 'Go fugg yourself!'

Serrano had laughed and slammed the door shut. 'Give him some water,' Slaughter had heard him say. 'Keep him alive. He may be of use to us.'

A while later he heard the sounds outside of men mounting horses, and the thudding of hooves as they galloped off. If he was to act it would have to be fast. He recalled Raoul's spurs raking across his chest in a final vindictive blow when he had thrown him in here. He did not relish any more of his medicine. Slaughter looked around him, but there was no bunk, no bucket, nothing he could use as a weapon.

Just plain solid adobe walls, a thick oak door, and a floor made from a mixture of river sand, bullocks' blood and cactus juice, which had hardened like concrete.

Slaughter winced as he examined the razor-thin cuts streaking his chest and arms, received as he tried to protect himself from Raoul. His thoughts lurched back and forth as he eased the torn, blood-caked shirt from sticking to his body.

'This were clean on yesterday,' he muttered. 'That bastard's askin' for trouble.'

His exhaustion seemed to pin him to the floor. His tongue was dry as dust and he thought of the water Raoul was supposed to bring him. Would he obey the order? In the dark recesses of the ceiling he spotted the cut-off stump of a pine beam jutting out over the door. It gave him a spark of hope. He gritted his teeth and forced himself to his feet. 'I gotta git up there.'

He got a foothold on the door hinge,

his fingernails hanging to the crack at its top and, gathering his fading strength made a superhuman grab for the pine beam. Then began the task of pulling himself upwards, his whole body trembling. Sweat trickled into his eyes, his mind told him it was no good, he had to let go. But no, he swung a foot up against the wall and twisted himself around until he was flattened against the ceiling above the door, holding himself aloft by the pole stub. He closed his eyes to try to conquer the sickness of pain stabbing through his side as a consequence of the sudden twisting movement. Finally it ebbed, and he looked down wondering how long he could stay up there defying gravity.

At last there was the echo of boot steps, spurs rattling, a man approaching. A key was turned in the lock, bolts were drawn, and the door creaked open. Below Slaughter, a greasy-haired head appeared, an arm holding a revolver, shoulders in an embroidered velvet jacket, another arm bearing a tin cup of water.

'Where the — ?'

They were the last words Raoul spoke. Slaughter dropped on him, crushing him to the floor, crashing the air from him. His fingers weaved into the greasy mop and he jerked up the skull, smashing it back down against the hard floor . . . again . . . and again . . . until he was lifeless. And then he squeezed the Mexican's windpipe until he heard it crack.

'So long, Raoul.' He stared at the water trickling away from the overturned mug. He made a grab at it and tipped a trickle of drops to his parched lips. Then he forced himself to get up from the dead man. Who else might there be around?

Slaughter took Raoul's revolver, a double action Smith & Wesson .44, and eased himself out of the cell. Holding onto the stone wall he staggered along the corridor until he reached the stairwell. 'Raoul, you there?' some man shouted in Spanish, and Slaughter saw his dark silhouette about to descend. He fired without hesitation and watched him tumble down.

'No, he ain't,' he growled.

He climbed over the prone body, and began to climb slowly, painfully, up the steps. The sun's blast hit him like a blow. He stood, blinking, looking about him, the S & W at the ready. Two shapes ran chattering with alarm from the doorway at the far end of the house. Instinctively Slaughter nearly fired at them, but realized in time that one was the fat black-clothed serving woman, Maria, and the other an equally corpulent man in greasy chef's outfit. He beckoned them to him with the gun.

'Who else is around?' he asked in his rough Spanish.

'No one, *señor*. They have gone into town.'

'Go get me a horse. And don't try any tricks or she gets it.'

The chef scuttled off to do as he was

bid and duly returned with a saddled mustang. 'Now, you're gonna have to help me up on this.'

By another superhuman effort, in his state, he climbed into the saddle and the mustang went weaving away. He did not seem to have the power to control it. It was all he could do to stay in the saddle as the pain creased through him, and they went jogging away. The cook and serving woman watched him go and shrugged. They were glad to be still alive.

But Slaughter was not in good shape. The horizon was wavering up and down like some desert mirage. The loss of blood, the pain, had made him light-headed. He could not stay upright. He slumped forward and hung, desperately, around the horse's neck. Alarmed, the mustang kicked and bucked, and went galloping across the deserted plain at the front of the house, through the clumps of grazing longhorns, scattering them, until it reached the scrub of cacti and thorns and rocks. The mustang went leaping and weaving up through the great rocks, bent on escaping this man hanging around his neck, to be free of the scent of blood. The mustang was halfway up the hill when he finally shook the man free, whinnied, and raced away.

Slaughter hit the ground hard and heard his own breath escaping from his lips in a gurgling groan. His head had connected with a rock. He knew that. He looked up at the mercilessly burning sun. The ground was spinning under him, whirling him around, faster, faster, until he remembered no more.

★ ★ ★

When he got back to his *hacienda*, the *Rancho Tejon*, and found Slaughter missing and two of his most efficient *vaqueros* lying dead, Serrano took out his fury on his cook, smashing him in the face with his fist. 'Why didn't you stop him?' he shouted.

'*Señor*, what could I do?' the overweight chef wailed. 'He had a gun in his hand. He rode away on a horse.'

'He can't have got far in that state,' Serrano ranted, hurling a bottle to smash the kitchen pots. 'You men, what are you standing there for? After him! A hundred silver dollars to the man who brings me his head.'

But the trail of the escaped prisoner petered out. The stolen horse was found wandering ten miles away. As for Slaughter, the earth appeared to have swallowed him up.

Maybe somebody had found him and taken him back to San Andreas? Or maybe — he was one tough *hombre* — he had been strong enough to steal another horse and make his way across the border? It was a mystery.

Five days later, news came that Rose Turner had put her ranch up for auction. She had advertised it in the San Andreas *Citizen*, a cheap two-page news sheet, and on billboards in the town. The sale was to be held on the Monday next.

Only a sprinkling of bidders turned up at the ranch on auction day, and half of them were only there out of nosiness to see what was going on. They poked around the barns, the wagon shed, and corrals, and even pushed their way into the house to take a look. Rose Turner stood about, her arms folded, as if resigned to her fate.

'Who will start me off at twenty thousand?' Lawyer Skinner, in his other hat as auctioneer, shouted, as he stood on a wagon. Nobody replied. 'Gentlemen there are more than two thousand head of stock out on the range, you know that. Beef prices are high. The stock alone would fetch thirty thousand dollars in Kansas. Or twenty thousand for the army contract in Tucson.'

A burly, bearded rancher from Tucson way, name of Williams, in a tall Stetson and long duster coat, tipped his finger. 'I'll go ten thousand the whole caboodle.'

'Gentlemen, don't let's be absurd. Miss Turner has put a reserve price of fifteen thousand on the whole place, lock, stock and barrel. Y'all know it's worth twice that.'

'This place is unlucky,' a woman squawked. 'You'd be well advised to take his ten thousand, Miz Turner.'

Rose's heart fell when she saw Jesus del Muchado Serrano come trotting into the ranch on his white stallion, followed by eight of his men. And he appeared to have heard the woman's remark.

'Unlucky?' he called, flashing a smile. 'You can say that again, *señora*. This place has been cursed. It has been plagued by *bandidos*. In my opinion it is practically worthless.'

The small crowd fell sullenly silent. They had their own ideas about who the *bandidos* might be, but they weren't about to say so. Williams wasn't from these parts. 'OK,' he said. 'I ain't interested in the land. I'll give you fifteen thousand for the stock.'

Serrano's *vaqueros* were as evil a bunch of desperadoes to be seen, even in Arizona Territory. They were the flotsam of the prisons, or rapists, thugs, murderers who had crossed the border to escape the *Federales*. All Serrano required was that they could use rope, gun, whip or knife to fine effect, and obeyed orders. In return he gave them a handful of silver dollars each day, beef to eat, and mescal to drink.

Without hurry, two of them swung from their mustangs beside Williams. One, Manolo, was as tall as the cattle buyer, a great gut bursting the buttons of his greasy shirt, two bandoliers of bullets criss-crossed over his shoulders. The brim of his sombrero tipped that of Williams's Stetson as he leaned one arm on his shoulder, eased a revolver from his holster and growled in his ear, 'Fifteen thousand? I don' theenk you got that much, meester. Mebbe you theenk about thees again?'

The *vaquero* on the other side was

as thin as his *compadre* was broad. He had taken a vicious-looking knife from his belt and was testing it on his palm. His elbow accidentally nudged the rancher. 'Mebbe your bid ees not good idea?'

Williams's mouth gaped and he tugged at his beard. He stared at the rest of Serrano's men who had gone to take up positions lounged against the auctioneer's wagon and, their hands toying with revolvers and carbines, were intently watching the small crowd.

'Hey!' Ben Turner shouted. 'What's this? A setup? Mr Skinner, these men have no interest in bidding. Get them out of here.'

'Just how do I do that, Ben? They got a right to watch proceedings if they want.'

'Of course they have,' Serrano said. 'Roseta, I suggest you forget about your reserve. Throw the sale open. I will start the bidding at two hundred dollars.' He doffed a hand to the crowd and smiled. 'Anybody going to beat that?'

A farmer's wife shouted, 'Sure, I'll go two fifty fer the house and contents,' but her husband shook her arm. 'Shut up, woman, you ain't bidding nuthin'.'

'I ignore that ridiculous suggestion,' Skinner said. 'Mr Williams has bid us fifteen thousand. Who'll give me sixteen thousand? Come on ladies and gents, don't be shy.'

'I just remembered.' Williams scratched at the back of his hair with considerable embarrassment as Manolo whispered in his ear again. 'I'll have to withdraw that bid. I ain't got that much in the bank. I better be goin' now. I got another appointment someplace.'

The rest of the crowd muttered and began to stir and move away. 'Friends,' Ben shouted, 'don't be intimidated by these men. This is a free country. They can't ride roughshod over us like this.'

'I'm sorry, Ben.' A rancher from the far end of the valley touched his arm.

'We don't want no trouble. You better sell your cattle in Tucson, stick the place up for sale.'

Other townspeople and farmers glanced, guiltily, Rose's way, and began to drift off, climbing into their buggies, and onto their horses, heading away.

'You lousy bastard,' Ben shouted at Serrano, throwing aside the lapels of his suit, his hands over the twin revolvers on his belt. 'You're pure evil.'

Serrano patted the butt of his carbine in his saddle boot, and looked down from the white stallion with a smile. 'You know how to use those pistols, Ben? Or are they just a bluff?'

'You want to find out?'

'Don't Ben,' Rose cried out, sharply.

Serrano glanced at her, and at his men taking up positions ready to blast the young dude. 'I'd back a carbine against pistols any day,' he whispered, throatily. 'You want to prove me wrong?'

'You won't do anything.' Rose stepped forward to stand in front of her brother. 'You've done enough. Get off my land before I get my own gun.'

Serrano gave a high-pitched nervous laugh. 'Look at her protecting her little brother. Come on, boys, I got the feelin' we ain't wanted here.'

He spurred the white stallion away, and his men went to leap on their own mustangs, whirling them in the dust, riding away after him.

Ben heard Serrano's mocking laughter drifting back on the breeze. 'You should have let me have it out with him, Rose. It would have been me or him.'

'Don't be silly, you wouldn't have had a chance. They would have made mincemeat of you.'

'Rose is right. You ain't a shootist, boy,' Skinner said, patting his shoulder. 'You're a writer, aincha? That's where your power is. Why doncha put something about this in one of the big Tucson papers? Bring people's attention to what's going on in these parts.

Maybe then they'll send a marshal down to sort things out.'

'I'm afraid it might be too late by then,' Ben replied. 'But I guess I could give it a try.'

8

'Where am I?' Slaughter said when he woke and met the green-flecked eyes of a young Mexican girl. 'Never thought I'd get to heaven. You one of them angels?'

'Shush.' The girl was gently bathing the swollen bruises and cuts on his face, and she certainly had the healing touch of an angel. 'You are with friends.'

'Anyone who is an enemy of Jesus Serrano is a friend of ours.' A middle-aged man, thin and gaunt in the ragged pyjama costume of the average *peon* was sitting cross-legged on the dusty floor of a gloomy cave lit by a candle stub. 'His men have been searching for you. That is why we brought you up here on the mountainside. They do not know this place.'

The girl's eyes were luscent in the

candlelight, which glowed on the black sheen of her hair, drawn severely back beneath her coarse-woven *reboso*, the peasant female's all-purpose shawl.

'Can you sit up, *señor*?'

'Sure.' He groaned as he did so from the sudden stab of pain in his ribs, but was grateful for the cooling drops of water in his mouth from the clay *olla* she held. His mind still felt muzzy, spinning feverishly, and he asked, 'What happened?'

'We saw you come riding from the *hacienda* and fall from the horse. We guessed you were no friend of the men who live there. We had heard gunfire,' the man said. 'We got you onto our pack-jack and brought you here.'

'No, they ain't no friends of mine. I did for a coupla the varmints. No different to me than killing a coupla rats.'

For some reason the girl crossed herself, hurriedly. 'There is too much death in this valley since Jesus arrived. It is a blasphemy that he should use our Saviour's name.'

'Yeah, he sure ain't the harbinger of goodness and love.' He reached for the *olla*. 'Here, I can manage this, honey.' The water was like a blessing and he drank deeply, poured a little over his face. 'That's good.'

'Lie back,' the girl commanded. 'I will wash the wounds on your chest.'

Slaughter gasped as she washed the gashes inflicted by Raoul's spurs, and from the rocks he had been dragged over. The leather chaps had taken the brunt of the punishment to his legs, but there was a pain throbbing in one ankle. 'Well, you must be an angel in human form,' he said, and touched her slim arm. 'You sure are a pretty li'l chickadee.'

A peach-coloured blush rose to the oval cheeks of her Spanish-brown face. 'Lie still, *señor*.' She began to pick away the torn blood-caked shirt to reveal his wide, hair-matted chest, the muscled abdomen which had taken their blows without too much trouble.

She soaked a rag and dabbed at the open cuts. 'You need to see a doctor. These are bad.'

'Aw, I'll be OK. Mebbe a coupla ribs cracked.'

Her father had torn up some strips of rags. 'We can bind you with this,' he said. 'The only doctor in these parts is the *brujo*.'

'Oh, yeah, the witch doctor with his rattle and herbs and powdered snake flesh. No, I'll give him a miss, thanks.'

'He has his benefits. Ancient lore modern man knows little of,' the father said. 'But mostly you need faith in him.'

'Or her,' the girl put in.

Slaughter grunted as they sat him up and bound him tight with the rag bandages. 'Well, seein' as you're doin' such a good job maybe you could take a look at my left ankle.'

The man eased his boot off, with difficulty, for the ankle was badly swollen. 'Can you move your foot?'

'Yeah, sorta. I guess it's just a sprain, thank God.'

'Thank Him, indeed, *señor*.' The father deftly wrapped a damp rag tight around his ankle. 'If so, all you need is to rest.'

'I gotta git going. I don't know what that hyaena's up to, but I've the feeling it's something pretty lousy.'

'What is your quarrel with Serrano, *señor*?'

'Apart from this' — he indicated his injuries — 'I got paid to protect a young woman and I ain't done a very good job of it. You know Rose Turner?'

'*Si*, she ranches on the far side of the river. I say know, but she was only a child. I knew her father.'

'You know Serrano has been rustling her stock, persecuting her?'

'*Si*, but what can an ordinary *peon* do about this? I herd my few sheep; I look the other way; I stay silent when those men ride by: it is the only way to survive.'

'You know, you don't strike me as an ordinary *peon*.' Slaughter lay back and was pleasantly surprised to find his tobacco pouch in his jeans' pocket. He stuck a paper on his lower lip and began to roll a quirly. The girl offered him a light from the candle and he lit up, smiling at her. 'For a start, no ordinary peasant and his daughter speak such good English.'

'It is best you do not know, *señor*, about us.' The man stood and, in spite of the worn *huaraches* on his bare feet, his battered straw hat, there was something aristocratic about his bearing. 'I am a shepherd in Serrano's employ. We will tend you here until the hue and cry is over. Then you must go, say nothing of us. Our lives depend on your silence.'

'You can depend on that. I ain't likely to go blabbing to Serrano. Anyway, my thanks to you, *amigos*.' Slaughter reached out for the Smith & Wesson revolver they had laid nearby, and twirled the cylinder with a thumb.

There were four bullets left. 'Don't leave it too long until you return. I git lonesome.'

'We will come in the morning with some food. Come, Dorothea.'

'We will pray for you,' the girl smiled, and slipped out after him.

'Yeah, that should help.' Slaughter lay and stared at the gaunt rocks for a while, pondering about the man and his daughter. He doused the candle to save it. He guessed all he could do was try to get some sleep, get his strength back. He had lost a lot of blood.

★ ★ ★

Several days passed and time dragged. He would hop to the entrance of the cave and look out over the ragged land. On one occasion he saw a band of *vaqueros* passing close by. There were shrill cries as they descended on what appeared to be a lean-to of rocks and wood built against a cliff wall about half a mile away down the slope. There was a stone corral full of scraggy sheep. There were shouts and it looked as if the girl and her father were being questioned by the *vaqueros*.

'Huccome they don't give 'em the treatment?' the gunfighter wondered. 'They got ways to make 'em squeal. If I was that gal's father I wouldn't be very happy about her safety, least to say, her virginity. Maybe there's some honour among thieves? The Mexicans are a funny bunch.'

Sometimes the father would arrive after dark, sometimes he would have Dorothea with him. He did not seem to trust this hired gun to be alone with her. 'I am sorry we have little to offer you,' the man said, handing him a piece of cheese, thin Mexican tortillas, a can of sheep's milk.

'Thass OK. I'm grateful for this.' Slaughter ate, hungrily. From his travels south of the border he well knew the desperate poverty of the ordinary *peon*, the high infant mortality rate, the early deaths due to poor diet and disease.

A family who owned a pack-jack, a patch of corn, and a few fowls were considered prosperous. 'You ain't given me your handle yet, *amigo*. Mine's James Slaughter. I'm in your debt.' He stuck out his hand.

'It is best you do not know my name.' However, the man offered a firm grip. 'It would not be wise.'

'Aw, come on. It won't go no further. Who *are* you?'

The Mexican took a goatskin vessel from his shoulder, unplugged it, and tipped it to his mouth. He swallowed the jet of pale liquid and winced. He wiped the top with his palm, and offered it to the American. 'Drink, *señor*. You are not pure Anglo, are you?'

'Nope. I got some Injin in me. Most people on the frontier have. Goes back to my grandmammy. From what I heard she was raped by Comanches. I was brought up in white ways, fought for the Texas Brigade in the white man's war. I guess I'm a quarter-breed.

Thass my story. So about you?'

'Sometimes it is good to talk.' The father watched Slaughter take a good drink of the mescal, give a stunned shake of his head and hand it back. He poured another trickle into his own mouth. 'Sometimes this loosens the tongue. I have your promise what I tell you will go no further?' When Slaughter nodded, he announced. 'My name is Serrano. Does that surprise you?'

'Yeah.' Slaughter blinked. The mescal homebrew was powerful stuff. 'I guess it does.'

'Francisco del Muchado Serrano, at your service. Jesus is my nephew. He is the son of my late brother who was what you might call the black sheep of the family, a worthless, drunken drifter, robber, fraudster and general bad lot. He always envied me my estate. I offered to take him as a partner, but it was no good. He would not work. He was too fond of liquor, the easy life. Jesus takes after him. He is not a slave to liquor' — he doffed the goatskin — 'but he is a terrible hard man, as you well know.'

'So, huccome he's living in a *hacienda* and you're in a hovel on the mountainside tending a few sheep which, I presume, belong to him?'

'Yes, he keeps careful watch. I am not allowed to kill one to eat. All have to be accounted for.'

'The *hacienda*, all that land belongs to my father,' Dorothea burst out. 'We lived there happily for many years before my mother died. Then *he* arrived.'

'You mean he just turned up one day and took over?' Slaughter said. 'Why didn't you resist? Why didn't you bring the law in?'

'Ha! The law!' Francisco Serrano scoffed. 'What do the *Americanos* care if we Mexicans fight among ourselves? I did resist. Oh, yes, we fought. He and his prison scum killed most of my men, ran the others off. He threatened to kill Dorothea, too, forced me to hand over the deeds to the estate.'

'Very neat. So that's how he got control? I thought he had the instincts of a pirate.' Slaughter gave a low whistle. 'Waal, whaddaya know. Our friend Jesus ain't only a rustler, a torturer, well-poisoner and murderer, he's an imposter, too.'

'That is right, *señor*. He allows me to work for him, to run a few sheep for a starvation pittance. It seems to amuse him, whenever he passes by, sees me in rags. I suppose there is a bitter irony.'

'Why don't you run away, protest to someone?'

'Where would we go? We are destitute. At least we are still on our own land. As long as we behave we have his protection — for a while.'

'For a while?' Slaughter glanced at the girl and saw the thrust of her breasts against the thin blouse, the slim shapeliness of her bronzed bare legs protruding from the skirt. He saw, too, a sliver of fear in her eyes. 'You mean — ?'

'Yes, my daughter has turned into a very attractive girl. Already the *vaqueros* have been pestering her, but they dare not do anything. Jesus is of our blood. He has given us our lives if we remain silent. But, I fear' — he lowered his voice — 'he has had no luck with the Turner woman. I fear he may soon turn his attentions to Dorothea.'

The girl had overheard. 'I would never give in to him,' she spat out. 'I would rather die.'

'I fear men like Jesus Serrano take whatever they want,' her father muttered. 'They do not ask.'

'Yeah, he's a real bad boy. So, you're kinda living on a knife edge?'

'I am, *señor*. If I had any honour I would kill him, myself. But I fear I would not succeed. And if I tried to run away I believe he would not let us get far. He has robbed me of my courage and of my honour. I am at my wits' end what do to.'

'Don't worry, Papa. I don't think even Jesus is so bad a man he would hurt me. I *am* his cousin.'

The two men's eyes clinched but they remained silent. Both knew that Jesus Serrano was a man who would take extreme pleasure in such evil.

'Somebody's got to stop that feller,' James Slaughter muttered. 'And it looks like it's down to me.' He stared gloomily at his useless ankle. He still couldn't bear to put any pressure on it and had come to fear that it was probably broken. 'But I ain't much good to anyone in this condition. Might jest as well put a slug in my brain like some damn useless horse.'

'Cheer up,' Dorothea smiled. 'Maybe we can fetch you help.'

9

Gunshots crashed out, echoing off the sun-warmed red wall of the rock known as Mexican Hat which reared up dwarfing the puny man-made structures of the ranch buildings. The sound, like a cachinnation of laughter, shattered the deathly silence of siesta time. 'That's better,' Rose Turner breathed out, hanging on to the hot cylinder of her father's old Dragoon revolver. 'I got two of them.'

'*Muy buen, señorita*! One of her new cowboys, Eusebio, was sitting in the shade of the rock, and gave her a mocking smile. 'But you will have to do better than that against Señor Serrano.'

Rose gave an involuntary shudder at the name. But, it was true. Two of the stones she had placed on the rock wall were missing, her other four bullets gone wide. Although she had been taught to use a lightweight hunting rifle as a girl, she had never fired the powerful, .45 calibre handgun before. Even if she grasped it with both hands the long-barrelled weapon was so heavy her aim wavered, and the recoil jerked it upwards. There were some tasks a female's smaller, weaker physique was not cut out for, and this was one of them.

'If that hypocritical crocodile comes sneaking around here again I'll blow him to smithereens,' she said, but she was far from certain she would have the nerve to fire at a man, any man, let alone Jesus Serrano, who was known to be a fast and accurate marksman.

'Aim at his belt buckle,' Eusebio called across in Spanish. 'Imagine him standing there. Aim eight inches below where you want to hit.'

'Aim like you really want to hit him,' his comrade, Rodrigo, joined in. 'If you going to use a pistol you got to be ready to kill.'

'I am doing,' Rose gritted out, as she emptied the cylinder and reloaded. The old-fashioned ball and cap Dragoon had been converted by the Thuer system to take the new centre fire brass cartridges. 'Maybe I should buy a lighter gun.'

Eusebio had got to his feet to languidly replace the stones, and returned to the shade. When the two *vaqueros* who rode for Serrano had turned up at the ranch earlier in the day, Rose had greeted them warily, with the heavy Winchester rifle in her hands. But they told her they were deserters from his band.

'We do not like what he is doing,' Eusebio had said. 'The rustling, well, that is fair enough. But when he poisoned the water, when he tortured the *Americano*. Heuch!' He made an expression of disgust and spat in the dust. 'We have had enough.'

At first she had not trusted them and told them to clear out. They might have been sent to spy on her, or who knew what. But she had relented, for she needed *charros* and Anglo ones were impossible to recruit now word had got about. They were two younger ones of Serrano's men, just a couple of easy-going drifters, who had robbed a bank and been chased over the border by the *Federales*. When they joined Serrano, they claimed, they did not know what they were getting into.

'I guess that's enough practice for today.' Rose returned the Dragoon to the holster of the gunbelt she had strapped around the waist of her skirt. It was heavy and awkward to wear, but she had determined to be ready to fight. 'Go get your horses saddled,' she said. 'My brother's down at the cow camp. I'll take you along and explain that you're on the payroll.'

If they were reliable they were a gain. It was a bit like a chess game, taking two of her opponent's pawns. With nine of his others knocked out he would soon need to go recruit more men. Eusebio had told her of Serrano's anger when he returned to find two of his *vaqueros* dead, and of James Slaughter's disappearance.

'At least he's alive,' she murmured, as she stood at the base of the rock on its rise and looked out across the great basin that stretched away into a grey-purple distance to a southerly horizon of sharp-cut peaks of mountain ranges against a crystal-clear sky. 'I wonder what he's up to?'

Not that she gave a damn, she reminded herself, about that surly, rude, insolent man-hunter, but she was glad Serrano had been unable to carry out his vile threat. She wouldn't wish that on any man.

Nor did she really wish to leave this land. It was cruelly arid, peopled by some heartless men, hard as the land itself. Saguaro, barrel cactus, creosote bush, smoke tree, great tumbled rocks: it spread out before her, the superimposed outlines of the successive and intercutting mountain ranges merging into paler planes of blue.

It was an effect of light most

noticeable at this time of late afternoon, a luminous and enchanting one. There was such a silence and serenity about the scene — at least, there *had* been, before this trouble arose — the greens, sand yellows, and rock reds of the valley stretching across the river for some twenty-five miles, the Turner ranch on its benchland on the north side and the far-off Serrano *hacienda* on the other. And dominating the panorama of mountains that ringed the horizon was the tall sacred peak of Baboquivari, sacred to the Papago indians, that was. It was a beautiful land. It was her home. No, she would not, could not, leave.

'*Señorita*!' Eusebio's shrill shout interrupted her contemplation of the scene. He was riding his mustang up towards her, leading her ready-saddled bay gelding. 'We are ready to go when you are.'

'I was just thinking,' she murmured, more to herself, 'that I am grateful to Señor Serrano for interrupting the auction. I am glad I did not sell. I do not want to.'

He had stepped down and she accepted his offer of cupped hands to put her foot in to mount the bay. She slipped into the saddle, sitting sideways in her long skirt, and led them down to the ranch house. 'Wait for me,' she said. 'I need to freshen up.'

She visited the privy at the back, which was never a very pleasant place to be, with its buzzing flies and lurking spiders. She went back into the washhouse and filled a bowl with water. She stripped off her blouse and splashed at her face, at her breasts and underarms. While she was so engaged, Juanita, the woman who helped with the cooking and house-keeping, bustled in, and offered her a clean towel.

'God bless us!' she seemed to be struck with sudden admiration. 'The *señorita* is beautiful. Why are you not married yet? You deprive a good man of much pleasure. You should have many children.'

'I have not yet found a good man,' Rose smiled, drying herself. 'Maybe one day.'

'The *señorita* has been disappointed in love. Do not let that deter you. It will give you wisdom to choose wisely. The second love is often the sweeter and the one long-lasting.'

'Hmm?' Rose said. 'The trouble is there's not a lot to choose from.'

She went to her bedroom and found a fresh bodice and blouse in the drawer. She brushed her dark mane of hair and glanced in the glass. Yes, her Spanish origin was a tad apparent. The high cut of her cheek, a certain haughtiness to her brow and delicately chiselled nose. Unlike most Mexicans, who were Indian-dark, or olive complexioned, her skin always remained pale, and so clear one could see the blue veins at the temples. This she owed to her mother, who, it was said, had royal blood. She had been an eligible, much sought after socialite in Mexico City; in fact, promised by her family to a prominent member of President Diaz's regime. Her father had met her at an embassy ball. He had owned a mine in Mexico at the time. It had, apparently, been love at first sight. They had been forced to elope and flee north of the border to escape Diaz's vengeance. It was then her father had bought this land north of the Diablo and fought the vengeance of the Apache, instead. Her mother had died in one of their attacks from a poisoned arrow. So, both her parents were dead now and it was up to her to carry on.

Rose sat on her bed for a few moments and thought about Maria's words. Yes, she loved children, and she had always hoped to have one or two of her own. But she had been kept apart from other girls of her age. She had grown up innocently unaware of the mechanics of the business. In her early teens she had always had the idea that when she married she and her husband would go to see the local doctor and he would supervise their conjunction and that would be it. How innocent could she be! Recently she had come to realize that this business with men could be far more brutal. Her thoughts lingered on the incident with James Slaughter . . . her stunned shock at the sight of him rising from the tub . . . the confusion of the fall in the splashing suds . . . and even then it was as if she were hypnotized. He had just lain there, that flicker of amusement in his eyes, the husky mocking drawl, 'What's the matter. Ain't you never seen one afore? Don't worry, all men's ain't as grand as this. I'm one of the lucky ones!'

All Rose knew of males before was sharing the tub with her brother until the age of ten. Even Jesus Serrano, although they had kissed and caressed, was in some ways a gentleman. He had never unveiled himself so blatantly. Possibly he had bottled up his lust until it had finally burst and he had attacked her. But she had escaped that 'fate worse than death,' as young women of good family considered it. In fact, she had had two lucky escapes. So why did the gunman's mulish laughter still echo so tantalizingly in her mind, making her blush for her thoughts? Why was she even thinking about him?

Rose hurriedly pulled on soft leather riding boots, grabbed her whip, and strode out onto the veranda. Hopefully, soon, she would meet a decent man and such desires would be properly constrained within the love and sanctity of marriage. Soon she would have to break free of this nightmare, even if it meant she, herself, would have to shoot Serrano. Then the hateful *Americano* could go on his way. And life would return to normal.

'Yes,' she cried, thrusting the rifle into the saddle boot, notching her revolver belt again. 'Let's ride.' She balanced herself side-saddle and went racing out of the ranch and across the sage brush followed by the two *vaqueros*.

10

'Howdy,' Slaughter growled, as he pushed his head through the antelope skin flap covering the doorway of the lean-to. 'Thought I'd make a social call. Is that frying *tamales* I can smell?'

'What are you doing here?' Francisco Serrano demanded, kneeling upright, with surprise, from his position on the earth floor. '*Señor*, you endanger both yourself and us.'

His daughter, Dorothea, was kneeling over the slow-burning embers of a mesquite fire tending to their supper in an iron frying-pan. She looked up with a smile. 'We were going to visit you later with some food.'

'Aw, I got pissed off lyin' in that cave all day and night. I've got shack fever. I gotta git out. I made myself a kinda crutch with a stick. They oughta call me Hop-along. It sure is good to be on the move under the stars.'

'My nephew's men have been nosing round. I believe they are suspicious. It was too dangerous to come to you in the daylight.'

'Yeah, I saw 'em.' Slaughter shivered, either from his wounds, or the night cold. He was only wearing the ragged remains of his blood-caked shirt. 'What's going on? Any idea?'

'From what I overheard I believe Jesus Serrano has driven the cattle rustled from Miss Turner south to Lukeville to sell. Or maybe across the border to Sonoyta. That town is a den of thieves. The brands would be too distinctive to sell in Tucson. He has taken most of his men and plans to enlist more. He has left just a couple of *vaqueros* guarding the *hacienda*.'

'Good.' The roof of the triangular-shaped *hogan* was almost too low to stand without stooping and Slaughter hopped along beside Dorothea to warm himself at the fire. 'Maybe now would be an ideal time to get in and retrieve my gun and my bronc? I've had 'em a long time. I kinda got the feel of 'em.'

'I do not think that would be a good idea, *señor*.'

'Waal, if it weren't for this durn foot I would. How far away's the *hacienda*? About ten miles? It would take me most the night to hop that far. And I wouldn't be too agile if they started taking pot-shots at me. I just got four slugs left.'

'No, I think it best you rest your foot another week or two. And then get out. Forget about your horse, your gun, forget us, forget all this. Go far away. There must be plenty more men you can pursue for money.'

'What's wrong with you, Mr Serrano? You like living like a slave, in poverty, at the mercy of that man? What's happened to your guts?'

'Don't speak to my father like that,' the girl cried. 'It is my safety he is thinking of.'

'Yeah, well, so am I. And someone

else's. And there ain't no safety while he's around.'

'We don't want trouble. We can manage as we are.'

'Yeah? Uh — thanks.' Slaughter accepted a tin plate of chilli-flavoured *tamale* and what looked like fried beans and prickly pear. He squatted down, eating hungrily, and glanced around at the firelit hovel. It was constructed of rock and roofed with wide desert palm leaves and sticks. The only covering on the floor was a woven straw *petate*. Two bundles of rags and greasy sheepskins on either side obviously served as beds. An iron griddle, a few broken pots, a machete and *olla* for water were about the only possessions they had. It was little different to any other *peon*'s hut. 'You certainly ain't living in luxury. You really mean to tell me you were once *el gran padrone*?'

'That is so, *señor*.'

'Aw, why don't you call me Jim. What's all this *señor* crap? I ain't no better than you.' The gunman leaned back and picked a thorn from his gum as he digested the cheap food. 'Don't s'pose you got any of that mescal left, Francisco?'

'A little.' Serrano had a grey stubble on his lined, haughty face. Sometimes there was a cold gleam in his eye as he studied the *Americano*. Maybe, Slaughter thought, he might well have been an arrogant li'l cuss when he was *padrone*. It might have been poetic justice to make him see how the other half lived. It was the girl he wanted to help. He watched the older man get up in his raggedy clothes and find the goatskin hung up at the back of the hut. 'There we are, *señor*,' he said, as he offered it.

The repeated *señor* was like a drawn-out insult. He don't like me, Slaughter thought, as he let the mescal spurt down his throat. Mebbe he don't trust me. '*Salud*,' he growled, as he handed the goatskin back.

'With a li'l honey like you to protect I don't blame your daddy for being a bit shirty.' Slaughter gave a braying laugh, and caught hold of her slim arm with his hefty paw. He must have recovered his health for he was feeling mighty randy. Dorothea tugged her arm free and frowned at him before modestly lowering her eyes. 'Aw, thass OK. I know when a gal don't fancy me. I guess I'm a mite too old for you. Mebbe I'll have to go visit them whorehouse bitches after all.'

'Señor Jim.' Serrano's hand had moved towards the machete. 'Please do not touch my daughter.'

'Yeah, yeah. Look, you got a burro, aincha? Waal, I got a thousand dollars hid near here. It's yours for the beast. Take the cash and get out, take your gal someplace safe where you can start again. I'll head for the Rio Diablo on the jackass. I should be able to git there by sun-up. How's that hit you?'

Francisco Serrano hesitated. 'A thousand dollars for a *burro*? Are you really a crazy man? What do you want beside? What is the catch? Surely you do not think you can buy my girl?'

'I just wanna help you, fer Chris'sakes.' Slaughter spread his palms and snatched the skin of liquor back. 'Of course, I'll have to find where I stashed the damn cash first.'

The father and daughter crouched staring at him in the firelight as if he really were a madman. 'Hail,' Slaughter growled and took another swig. Suddenly he stiffened, raising a finger as he heard the sound of horsemen, the jingle of bridles.

'Ai-yai-yai-yee!' a man's voice shrilled out.

All three in the *hogan* froze and then Slaughter jerked his head at Francisco. 'Go see what they want,' he whispered.

There were two of them sitting their mustangs, darkly silhouetted against the stars, wide-brimmed sombreros, moonlight gleaming on their silver spurs, revolvers in their hands. Francisco looked up at them and asked, '*Señors*, what do you want?'

'What you theenk?' The light gleamed

on the gold teeth in the *vaquero*'s unshaven jaw, his thin, razor-sharp face. 'We come for your li'l *chiquita*. We wanna have some fun.'

The rider beside him was the big, fat, bearded one, Manolo, his rank smell announcing his presence before he had arrived. 'Why you wan' to keep her to yourself, old man? That ain't nice.'

'Get out of here, you spineless scum,' Francisco said. 'If Señor Serrano hears of this he will string you up. We have his protection. Surely you know that?'

'Yeah, I know that.' As well as unwashed flesh the big man also smelt of sweet rum and his words were slurred. 'But Señor Serrano ain't here, is he? Why should we care about him?'

'If you so much as touch my daughter he will put out your eyes with burning brands, I can guarantee that.'

'Yeah, but maybe we won't be here then,' Manolo sing-songed in a childish voice. 'We thinkin' of headin' back to Mexico.'

'Why argue with him?' The thin *vaquero* rode his horse forward, pushing Francisco aside, suddenly buffaloing him with his revolver butt. 'Let's get her!' He swung down from his saddle as Dorothea came through the door flap. He caught hold of her by her wrist as she tried to kneel down by her father.

'Leave me alone,' she screamed. 'What have you done to him?'

'He's OK.' The scrawny *bandido* caught the girl by her hair and dragged her back into him. 'He's taking a little nap, thassall. You don't do what I say you'll be taking a longer one. And him too.'

'Yeah,' the fat man roared. 'The long sleep you never wake from. How you like we slit your throats, both of you?'

Holding the girl by her hair so hard her eyes bulged, the thin one had holstered his revolver and his grimy hand was feeling for her breasts. 'How you like this, eh?'

'Don't, please,' Dorothea pleaded,

as he ripped her blouse apart, and her firm, nubile breasts were exposed. 'My father is speaking the truth. Jesus Serrano won't like it. I am promised to him.'

'Jesus won't be getting it,' the *vaquero* gloated, as his hand wandered and he tried to kiss her lips. 'Ouch,' he cried, as she bit into his lips and spat at him. 'You little whore.' He raised his fist to smack her —

'Hurry it up. It's my turn next,' Manolo was saying when James Slaughter appeared from the far end of the *hogan*. So intent was he on watching the girl he did not notice him standing there.

'Evening, gents,' Slaughter drawled. He already had the Smith & Wesson .44 raised and aimed at the thin one's head. He crashed out a slug and put him down while he had the chance, spattering the girl with blood.

'*Quién es?*' Manolo exclaimed, whirling his horse, blasting his revolver at the gunflash from the darkness.

But Slaughter had stepped aside, cocked the .44 with his thumb, and fired again. His bullet hit the fat man in his massive gut, and the *vaquero*'s face crumpled with amazed disbelief as he looked down and saw blood gushing through the fingers of his hand. He fired again, but his startled horse jumped, and the slug careered harmlessly away into the darkness. Slowly he toppled from his horse and crashed down to lie supine. Slaughter raised the smoking S & W and put another one into his heart to make sure.

'Look out,' the girl cried.

The thin *vaquero* was groaning on the ground minus half his jaw, but was reaching for his holstered gun. He had it half out when Slaughter's slug hit him again, spilling his brains this time.

They stood looking at the bloody corpses, a few moments before living, breathing men, the burning scent of sulphur in their nostrils, as the gunshots echoed across the valley.

'My aim's a tad out,' Slaughter said, looking at the .44 in his palm. 'This ain't much of a piece. I shoulda made sure of him first shot.'

Dorothea was standing, her lips trembling, staring at the sprawled men, trying to cover her bare nipples with her torn blouse.

'Aw, come on, it ain't so bad,' Slaughter growled, putting an arm around her and giving her a hug. 'Nobody ain't gonna miss 'em, thass for sure. An' I guess that nag's mighty relieved to be rid of him.' He glanced down at her and gave her another squeeze. 'Mm! Mighty nice li'l pair of prongs you got. I'm partial to a bit of tender breast, myself. Cain't really blame 'em for tryin'.'

The girl struggled away from him, as if she feared he might have the same designs as the *viciosos*, sobbing, backing away.

'I ain't gonna hurt yuh. You better take a look at your daddy. My guess is he's gonna have a mighty sore head in the mornin'.'

Dorothea frowned at him and knelt down beside her father, trying to gently wake him, while Slaughter turned over the fat man with his boot, and unbuckled his ammunition belt. He peered at the bearded face, the staring eyes. 'Ugly looking bastard, ain't he? It's a good job I decided to come callin'.'

'*Si*,' she said, '*gracias*. You saved our lives.'

'You did the same for me. Just repaying a debt.'

'I think you are a good man,' she smiled, 'in spite of your tough ways.'

'Waal.' The stone face furrowed into a smile. 'It's a long time since anyone said that to me.'

He bent down to take the other man's revolver and ammunition, and caught hold of their restless horses. 'One thing's for certain,' he muttered, as he peered out into the night. 'If there's any more of 'em around they'll sure know I'm here now.'

The father was coming round, leaning on one elbow, looking at them in a dazed way, as his daughter tended his bump with the *olla* of water and a rag. 'What happened?' he asked.

'Nuthin'.' Slaughter grinned. 'You'll be glad to hear.'

11

'The critical factor is water,' Ben Turner was saying, as they breakfasted by the chuckwagon. 'Each of these cows can drink up to thirty gallons a day. If we haven't got water, we're sunk' — his thin, boyish face split into a smile — 'to use an odd metaphor.'

'Waal, we ain't had none fer months.' Fat Bob raised a critical eye to the furnace-red dawn and the vast clear sky in the corner of which one little cloud could be seen. 'And it looks like it's going to be another oven-hot day.'

'The weather's gawn dang crazy ever since the War,' another 'puncher opined. 'I figger it's God's judgement on us.'

Rose Turner was seated on a rush mat among them, and could not refrain from smiling at the hand. 'What have you done to deserve such judgement, Hank?'

'It seems to me,' Ben put in, 'the weather's gone topsy-turvy since the buffalo disappeared. How many did there used to be, seventy-five million at a rough estimate? You cannot interfere with God's balance of nature like that without expecting repercussions.'

There had been a ten-year spate of terrible summer storms, downpours causing floods, washing bridges and whole towns away, carving through mountains and creating canyons where there had never been canyons before. And now this year had come the terrible prolonged drought.

'It looks like we're back to fourteen inches of rain a year,' Rose said.

'You're going to be in desperate trouble if the rains don't come,' Ben said. 'I won't mince my words. Now you've had the north water-hole poisoned we're totally reliant on this river, and just look at it.'

'We've got the well at the ranch,' Rose

replied, 'but that's hardly sufficient for our human needs.'

'There is water,' Ben said. 'There must be. Deep down under the tableland. What you've got to do, Rose, is make deep bore holes, maybe bring in heavy digging equipment, keep boring until you hit.'

'Perhaps I should employ one of those water diviners?'

'Perhaps. Yes, that's a good idea. They say there's an old Indian who's got the gift.'

'Well, at least we don't get any plagues of locusts any more like we used to. That's a blessing. Perhaps when the buffalo were killed they died off, too?'

'What I'm saying, Rose, is you've got to move fast. There's not enough in that river to water all these longhorns for much longer. What grass there is is as dry as hay and chawed to the ground. You'll have to move them out soon.'

Rose Turner tossed the dregs of her

coffee away and looked around at her few remaining men sprawled around like a circle of wolves chomping at their plates of beans and biscuits. They were as lean as the longhorns, worn out and darkly sunburned, with despondent expressions, forced to work long hours due to her shortage of men. By their grim expressions most of them seemed to privately think that the future for the Mexican Hat ranch was not good. She would not be surprised to wake in the morning to find a couple of them had packed up and gone.

'Well, it's good to get a couple more hands.' She glanced across at the two young Mexicans. 'You figure you can stand the hard work? I can only pay you twenty dollars a month, all found.'

'*Si*, you no worry,' Eusebio grinned. 'We like hard work. That Serrano, pah! He no good. Me an' Rodrigo, we don' like his ways.'

Rodrigo spun his revolver on a finger. '*Si*, we will be ready for him if he come.'

'The boys did pretty well yesterday,' Ben said. 'We got another four hundred head cut out and branded. But with what manpower we've got, Rose, I don't see us moving the whole herd. It's a damn hard drive and probably safest for us to go the long way round via the Gila. I think we should just take the four-year-old bulls and leave the cows and calves and young 'uns. That way you can rebuild the herd if you're really positive about staying.'

'Yes, I'm sorry to keep chopping and changing my mind,' Rose stood up, her tin plate and mug in hand to carry to the wagon. She stared across the river. 'He's not driving me out. I'm not turning tail. I'm going to stay and face him.'

'OK, boys,' Ben said, getting up to follow her. 'It's about time you got on them broncs of yours. We got work to do.'

'Oh, I nearly forgot. A letter came for you.' Rose went to reach into the saddle-bag of her bay gelding. 'It's from Kansas City.' She watched him open it and intently read, his pale face going, if possible, even paler. 'Anything wrong?'

'No.' He started, nervously, and read on. 'It's from Ruth.'

'Ruth?'

'Yes, the young lady schoolmarm I've been stepping out with.'

'I'm sorry. My mind's full of all this here. I forget you have your own life in Kansas, Ben.'

He stood in thought for a while, folded the letter and returned it to his pocket. 'It's a sort of ultimatum. She wants me to return at once. She wants *me* to make up *my* mind.'

'Marriage?'

'Yes. I have my career to think of, too. My editor's not happy about me taking this time off. I said I would only be a month. It's unpaid leave. But, it's six weeks gone already.'

'I'm really sorry, Ben.' Rose gripped his arm and stared at her brother. 'I'm so selfish. Here's me burdening you with my problems. You must go. I can manage. It was me decided I was going to keep the ranch going. It's down to me. Ben' — she hesitated, studying his expression — 'you really want to marry this girl, Ruth?'

'Yes, she's a fine girl. We have much in common. But, it seems, there's another admirer lurking in the wings. I had better get back, protect my interests.'

'Maybe she's just saying that? It seems a little odd to me. If she loves you she will wait, surely?'

He grinned at her. 'She's very headstrong. Look, what I'll do is help the men drive the bulls in to Tucson. I'll get as good a price for you as I can. I'll bank it for you. But then I think I had better catch the stage back to — '

Ben Turner paused as he spotted a Mexican girl on a *burro* weaving her way towards them through the rocks at the base of Tower Butte. She was wearing the typical *reboso* wound around her head and body, the robe used as shopping bag, baby carrier or shawl by Latino women. 'Where's *she* come from?'

As the girl drew nearer, and trotted her *burro* across the shallow river, he saw that she was extremely pretty, but with a rather fragile air. 'Hello,' he called. '*Buenas dias, señorita*. Can I help you?'

'Thanks to our Lady of Guadaloupe! I feared I would not find you. I have a message from the *Americano*.'

'The man called Slaughter?'

'*Si*, he was badly beaten but we have been caring for him.' She slipped from the wooden saddle and touched Ben's proffered hand. 'He wants you to come to him, to bring what men and rifles you can spare. You are Señor Ben Turner, are you not?'

'That's me.' Ben was transfixed by her sparkling eyes of greenflecks on brown, the dark pupils widening as they stared at him, the even wider whites. For some reason he felt as if a thunderbolt had hit him. He hung onto her hand, as if afraid this vision of loveliness might run away. 'May I ask your name?'

'Dorothea,' she said. 'Dorothea Serrano.'

'Serrano. Are you his sister?'

'No, he is my cousin.'

'What are you doing hanging onto her hand?' Rose asked. 'Come, let's give her a cup of coffee and a bite to eat.'

'First I must give the *burro* water. We have come a long way. It is difficult riding through the night.'

'I'll see to that,' Ben said. 'And a nosebag of split corn. His reward for bringing you here.'

While she ate breakfast, Dorothea explained to them about her father, about how Serrano had usurped their home, how he kept them in virtual slavery, threatening to punish them if they did not obey him. 'Once, for days, he refused to let us have water because my father would not do as he said. He is a cruel man. He enjoys humiliating us.'

'Is James — Mr Slaughter — is he OK?' Rose asked.

'*Si*, he is strong as an ox. He has made good recovery, apart from his finger and his foot. I have told him he needs proper treatment for them. The little finger is broken. I have tied it in splint. But the left ankle I am not sure of. He cannot put much pressure on it.'

Ben still appeared to be in a daze, constantly staring at the girl. 'Why . . . why?' he stuttered. 'Why does he want us to go to him?'

'Jesus Serrano has gone away. He has left the house unguarded. Señor Slaughter and my father have gone to take it back.'

'Take it back?' Rose exclaimed. 'That's a bit dangerous, isn't it?'

'*Si*, I think so, too. My cousin will return and he will no doubt have recruited many bad men. I do not see how they can hold out against them.

But my father is angry. He says he is tired of living like a slave.'

'Slaughter seems to have a death wish,' Rose said. 'You must have nothing to do with this, Ben. It is foolhardy to the extreme. You must take the beeves to Tucson, as we agreed, and return to Kansas to your ladyfriend. Get married, settle down, forget all this.'

'You have a sweetheart?' Dorothea asked, and there was a sudden sadness in her eyes. 'You live in Kansas?'

'Yes, he lives in a different world to us. A world of civilized people. Not this heathen frontier territory where men kill and torture with impunity. Do as I tell you, Ben. We're not getting involved in Slaughter's crazy schemes.'

'Hell take Kansas. This is my home.' Ben gripped the girl's hand once more. 'I'm going to help your father.'

'No!' Rose cried, sharply. 'What's the matter with you. Oh, good gracious! A pair of pretty eyes and a man takes leave of his senses.'

'They are indeed,' Ben said, for suddenly his schoolmarm ladyfriend did not seem so important. It was as if she had taken a back step into history. '*Very* pretty eyes, and eyes I could spend the rest of my life looking into.'

The peach blush rose to Dorothea's cheeks, and she smiled shyly at him. 'Perhaps you had better do as your sister suggests. I do not want to get you into trouble. It is true, there is danger. I begged my father not to.'

'There's danger in Kansas City. I could get run over by a horse-tram. First, I will ask the men if any of them are ready to volunteer. Then we will head for the *hacienda*.'

Rose raised her eyes and palms to the heavens in exasperation. 'Men! They just can't wait to kill each other.'

★ ★ ★

It took a while for them to locate in the moonlight the claw-shaped agave, with its huge twisted and tortured leaves. 'There it is,' the bounty hunter said, sitting astride Manolo, the fat man's mustang, with his bandoleer of bullets across his chest, his sombrero on his head, and in possession of his carbine. 'It should be under that rock. Make sure there ain't no heel-ah monster waiting to give you a bite.'

Francisco Serrano had got down from the other mustang to save Slaughter having to use his bad ankle. He poked in the hole with his captured rifle barrel, then gingerly put his hand in. He produced the wad of $1,000 in greenbacks wrapped in Slaughter's oilskin wallet to keep the termites out. 'There you are.'

'Keep it. Go catch up with your daughter, take her to safety.'

'No,' Francisco said, handing it to him. 'I am going with you. I am going to reclaim my home. It is I who should pay you.'

'Waal,' Slaughter grunted, tucking the wallet in the back pocket of his

Levis. 'That's up to you. I ain't so sure either of us is going to be gittin' outa this alive.'

'*Señor.*' The older man spoke proudly as he climbed on his mustang. 'We have a saying in Mexico. Better to die on your feet than live on your knees.'

'Yeah? Right, let's go. You know the best path?'

The dawn sky was flooding with crimson light as they approached the Rancho Tejon, its white stuccoed walls painted pink by the rays. If anybody else was left on guard they might well have thought the two riders, in their tall hats and ponchos, were Manolo and his *compadre* returning. They were nearly up to the gateway of the outer adobe wall when a shot rang out.

'*Pa-dang*! The bullet whined past Slaughter's head, making his bronc leap, wild-eyed.

'Hot damn,' he shouted, steadying the horse, which was high-stepping in fright. 'Get down behind the wall, Francisco. Give me time to git round the back of the house, then keep him as occupied as you can.'

He raked the bronc's sides with his spurs and spurted away as another bullet snarled past his head. He hung low and slapped the bronc's neck, galloping around the outer low wall. More bullets zipped past him like angry bees and he heard the crack of the rifle shots.

'Looks like he's on the flat roof,' he growled, when he reached the cover of the stabling. 'Seems like he's the only one here. What'll we do, hoss?'

The mustang had his own ideas about that and ambled in a hurry towards a row of clapboard stables behind the house. He was obviously glad to get home and went inside. Slaughter was pleased to see his liver and white-patch pinto, Cal, more like an old friend. He winked at him, made a shushing sound to try to keep him from whickering, and guided the mustang to the back of the stalls. He peeped through a crack in the boards.

There was the mansion's domed roof with two flat-roofed sections on either side. There was a low battlemented wall around each of them. The roof on the right side was where the gunman had been. There were holes punched in the wall as spyholes through which he could poke a rifle. But there was no sign or sound of anybody. It was going to be chancy crossing the stretch of bare ground to the *casa*, not knowing whether the guard might have him in his sights.

'What's happened to old man Serrano?' he muttered. 'Why ain't he shooting?' And an after-thought struck him with a jolt. 'Is he dead?'

Suddenly he saw a *vaquero* in a sombrero, white shirt and baggy pants show himself, crossing from the front of the roof to the back at a cautious crouch to peer around the precincts, going to the edge to peer down with his rifle in case anybody had got in close. Slaughter held the mustang steady with his knees and tried to poke the octagonal barrel of the old Sharps rifle he had taken from the thin *bandido* through a crack in the slats, but it stuck, and the mustang wouldn't hold steady. If the man on the roof scented him he wouldn't have a hell's chance — his bullets would smash right through the boards.

A rifle shot cracked out and the guard ducked and spun round as if to scamper back to the front of the house, disappearing from sight. Out at the front Francisco was letting loose with a volley of shots and the guard was replying. 'Here we go,' Slaughter muttered, pulling the mustang's head round and trotting him out of the stable. He crossed the dry stretch of sand, the Sharps at the ready, and halted him under the overhang by a kitchen door. He could either go through and up the stairs, or try another way. He chose that that would be the easiest on his foot. He returned the Sharps to the saddle holster, steadied his mustang, and eased himself up to balance, mainly on his right foot, on the saddle. It was now or never while the battle raged. He only hoped the horse didn't take it in his head to buck. He wobbled back and forth and made a grab to get a fingerhold in one of the portholes. His left-arm biceps bulged and strained as he pulled himself up almost until his chin was level with the hole, and he could glimpse the bandit lying down on the far side, firing his rifle. He reached with his right hand and hauled himself, rolling over the wall of the parapet to land on the roof.

'Hi!' Slaughter had the Smith & Wesson revolver in his hand, ready cocked as he lay there. He was never fond of shooting a man in the back. 'Hold it! Drop that rifle, mister.'

Either the guard did not understand English, or he was gun-crazed. He froze for moments, pushed the rifle away through the porthole, as ordered. But, then, he spun around and his hand was going for his Colt .45 tucked in his belt. *Ker-ash*! Slaughter's revolver boomed out. But a man in fear of his life can move like lightning. And this one was fast. Slaughter's first slug missed as the sallow-faced guard leaped, twisting to his feet, and the .45 was spurting flame.

It was Slaughter's turn to roll aside, without a split second to lose. The guard's slug smashed into the parapet wall behind him. Slaughter had done a complete revolution and had his .44 aimed again, beating the Mexican by another split second. This time he didn't miss. The guard tumbled back to lie propped against the low wall of the roof. A great splash of blood covered his chest and his eyes lost their fierce light. The revolver dangled from his lifeless hand.

'Phew! that was a close call, buddy,' Slaughter grunted. 'That might well have been me on the receiving end. Sometimes I figure I'm gitting too old for this game.'

He hopped across the roof as another of Francisco's shots clapped out and a bullet whistled past his head. He ducked down on his knees, raised his revolver and waved it back and forth. 'OK,' he yelled. 'It's over. Quit firing.'

He saw Francisco cautiously show his head. 'Come on over,' he shouted, raucously. 'He's dead.'

Slaughter wiped the sweat from his eyes and rested a few moments. He glanced at the dead man. The flies had already homed in on the wound and were buzzing, excitedly. 'Well, it's certainly all over for you, pal.'

12

'You think we oughta raise a flag, show you're in official residency again?' Slaughter greeted Serrano at the front door. 'There's another one down. There's only the cook and the maid at home.'

A smile spread out across Francisco Serrano's features, perhaps the first smile Slaughter had seen on his haggard face, as he stepped through the door and glanced around the great, shadowy banqueting room. He clapped his hands to the American's big shoulders. 'Thank you. This is a great day for me to stand here again. Thanks be to God, too.'

'Yeah? Well, some you lose, some you win. That's the way it goes, to and fro. One man's meat, another's poison, and so forth. But jest how long we're gonna be able to hold on to this place

I dunno. So you better make the most of it.'

'*Si*, indeed, yes. Thank you, Jim. Without you I would not have had the courage to try.'

'You would have had no chance, let's face it. A man's wise to stay low, wait his chance. So, that ole horn chair there used to belong to you? It's an impressive piece.'

'To me, to my father, to his father before him. Look, in case you doubt my word.' He strode over to the red rock fireplace, knelt down and eased out an adobe brick behind the mantel. He drew out a tin box from the secret place. From that he took a parchment scroll. 'It's still here. Jesus Serrano has only a modern copy of this. This is the deed granted to my ancestors by the King of Spain, this land to be held by my family in perpetuity.'

Slaughter took a look at the yellowed scroll. There was a lot of mumbo-jumbo that appeared to be in Latin written in an ornate hand, stamped with a royal seal, a magnificent coat of arms at the top. It was dated 1767, more than a hundred years before. 'It's all Greek to me. But it sure looks genuine. Hey, look, there's a map of this whole area. That's mighty int'restin' stuff. No sign of the Turner Ranch.'

'We owned their land, too. In fact, you could say we still have a right to it. Perhaps that is what bothers Jesus Serrano?'

'Waal, I ain't so sure any court would uphold that claim. Rights around here is what a man takes and holds onto. And the old Spanish law don't operate no more. Up in California hundreds of you old dons have been swindled out of your land by the new regime. But I guess this gives you fair entitlement to the Rancho Tejon.'

'Yes.' The old man's face returned to its customary solemnity as he studied the deeds. 'My only fear is, should I and my daughter die — God forbid! — Jesus Serrano might claim legal entitlement to this place.'

'Yeah, it's a wonder he's let you live so long.'

'Perhaps even he hesitates to kill his own blood relatives.'

'Somehow I doubt that. More likely he thought you'd never have the nerve to try to return.'

'Now I am back here I will never give this house up. Not while I've got life in my body.'

'That ain't exactly the wisest thing to say,' Slaughter muttered. 'Don't do to tempt fate. Aincha goin' to give me a tour of the place? We gotta see how best we can protect it.'

Don Francisco del Muchado Serrano led him around the rooms discoursing on their history. He showed the American his study and library. 'At least, in some ways Jesus Serrano is a cultured man. He has not vandalized the books and paintings and ancient artefacts. That is about all I can say for him.'

'They climbed up the stairs to the

gallery and inspected the bedrooms. In the lofty master bedroom there was a fine red cherrywood double bed, with a canopy and coat of arms over it. 'This must be where your nephew sleeps. I bet he sure fancied a romp in it with Rose Turner.'

'You know,' Francisco murmured, 'sometimes I think it would not be a bad idea if Jesus Serrano married Dorothea. At least our blood line would keep control of the *hacienda* and estate.'

'There's only one li'l problem to that, as I see it: she hates his guts.'

They wandered back down to the kitchen where Maria and the chef, Georgio, were busy preparing food. They turned with nervous eyes, and began bowing and kissing Don Francisco's hands. 'It is so good to have you back here, *señor*,' Maria cried.

'I think it might be wise for you two to take a little holiday as from tomorrow,' Francisco said. 'Go visit your families for a while. We can look after ourselves. Perhaps we will still be here when you return. Perhaps not.'

The cellars proved to be more of interest to James Slaughter. There were great barrels of red wine, port, sherry, whiskey and rum. Francisco found a cobwebby bottle of brandy on the shelf.

'He hasn't yet managed to drink all my finest stuff.' He pulled the cork, filled two glasses. 'To victory! To success!'

'Yeah! To oblivion. I'm gonna git pie-eyed tonight.'

'Didn't we ought to stand guard?'

'Sure, ole fella, you can do that. Me, I'm looking forward to a nice sleep in a feather bed. I might even take another bath. I kinda liked that last one.'

He had found a clean white linen shirt in the bedroom wardrobe. It was a trifle tight across his shoulders and, with its flounced front and ruffled cuffs, a tad pansyish for puritan American tastes, but certainly an improvement on his blood-caked shredded one. He tried on an embroidered velvet jacket, surprised how comfortable it was. He allowed Francisco to sit at the head of the table, but as he sprawled, tucking into canned lobsters, partridge in some kind of orange sauce, beef *chimichanges*, with rice, sweetcorn and red peppers, washed down by tumblers of rich red wine and brandies, balancing his bad foot on his spurs, Slaughter began to feel himself quite the don.

Soon he began to get muzzy-headed, and the brandy brought out the old malevolence in him. 'So,' he growled, 'I guess this is more to your taste than playing the shepherd, eh, 'cisco? I bet you could be a right bastard when you ran this place. How many *peons* did you have dragged in here to grovel before you? How many did you have flogged?'

Francisco Serrano stared at him, haughtily. 'There were times when I had to exert my authority. Sometimes it is the only way to be obeyed. But, as we say, a *peon*'s hide is hard. He can take the lash.'

'Yeah, I bet he can. It's a case of havin' to, ain't it? You ever go in for the chicken run? No? How about your seigneurial rights? How many little *señoritas* did you put in the family way.'

'That, sir, I did never do.' Francisco jumped to his feet. He, too, had dressed himself in a suit of pearl-buttoned velvet, boots and spurs, and a patterned shirt, and looked more of a nobleman. 'How dare you insult me?'

'Aw, siddown. You're a right banty li'l rooster. It ain't me you wanna fight. OK, I'll take that back. Here, have another drink.'

Francisco resumed his seat with a flurried look, tossing back his grey hair. He drank deeply, as if to catch up with Slaughter. 'It was probably my downfall that I was not strict *enough*, that I was too benevolent to my *charros* and servants. I would have been better advised to have hired a gang of *viciosos*, or, at least, harder men. Then we might have had more of a chance against Jesus Serrano.'

'You mean you were too, soft? Yeah, well, I guess you gotta try to strike a happy medium.'

'And when a man's only child is a daughter, this, too, has a softening influence.'

'But you managed to fight off the Apache?'

'Yes, we did. You can see the house is well-prepared for attack. The doors and shutters are solid oak, with ports for rifle fire. Put several good marksmen up on the roof behind the buttresses and you can hold off Indian attack.'

'Yeah, I guess.'

'Of course, I lost a good many of my best *vaqueros*, much stock, many valuable horses. And, then, when the Apache were on the run, chased into the mountains by the army, we were plagued by gangs of *Americano* drifters, the evil scalp-hunters. Apache scalps were worth one hundred dollars each. They were not choosy where they got them from. Many were the peaceful Indian villages which were descended on by those scum, men, women, children slaughtered.'

'Yeah, I heard about that. They talk about the blood-soaked soil of Tennessee, but it strikes me this land has seen its share of death.'

They were disturbed at their feast by the chef running in to say, with much agitation, '*Padrone*, horsemen are approaching!'

Slaughter stumbled, unsteady with brandy, and grabbed at a rifle. He staggered up to the roof and hopped across to one of the ports in the battlements, peering through. Sure enough, a spiral of dust betrayed the approach of horsemen. But they were coming from the direction of the Rio Diablo. 'Looks like Ben Turner and his boys,' he shouted, and muttered, as an afterthought, 'Just as well, I can hardly load this thang, let alone aim it.' His fingers appeared to have lost contact with his brain.

He hauled himself up onto the parapet as Ben and four cowboys, two of Mexican appearance, rode in, followed by a girl in a black shawl, side-saddle on a mustang. 'Aw, Jasus, what's she doin' here?' he groaned.

Don Francisco was asking the same question in irate Spanish of his daughter and Turner by the time Slaughter managed to hobble back downstairs, supporting himself on his rifle, his legs unsteady in spite of his ankle. He certainly needed support.

'She insisted on coming with us,' Ben was saying. 'I could not dissuade her. She said she had to be with her father.'

'Dang fool. Why dincha jest hog-tie the silly li'l bitch and leave her where she was — in safety?'

'I don't know. Yes, I'm sorry' — Ben seemed dumb-founded — 'I suppose I should have insisted. I never thought. She just jumped on a horse and followed us. Dorothea seems to have a very strong mind of her own.'

'Waal,' Slaughter drawled, slumping back onto a chair, and pouring another brandy. 'She's your problem. I guess; whoever wins this battle takes her, along with the house, as their prize.'

Ben visibly swallowed. 'I . . . I never thought of it like that. You mean we're really going to fight?'

'We sure are, boy. And the odds don't look good. So, maybe tomorrow you had better git on your hoss and hightail it back with her. Might be a good idea if you kept on goin' all the way to Kansas, and take her with you. She seems to have taken a fancy to you.'

Dorothea looked shyly at Ben and reached to hold his hand. 'We are not leaving,' she said. 'We have made up our minds. We are going to fight.'

'Right.' The gunfighter fondled the Schofield he had been reunited with. 'So, let's all have a drink to that.' Slaughter roared for Maria, the serving woman, to bring more glasses, and sloshed wine and brandy around. And the evening swept on in merriment and feasting as the others tucked into food at the long banqueting table. Eusebio, Ricardo, Hank and another cowboy, called Curly, had been quick to volunteer for this expedition. Three others, and Fat Bob, had been less eager, and it had been agreed they should remain and try to guard the herd, while Rose returned to the house.

'At least she's got some sense,' Slaughter growled, scowling at Dorothea. 'Wimmin, they jest get in the dang way if a man's got to fight.'

13

When he woke the next morning he felt as if he were suffocating. Something heavy, warm and soft was lying across his throat. He squinted to one side and saw it belonged to Maria, the serving woman. She had both her arms outstretched, cruciform, and was snoring, lustily.

'It musta been some party,' he growled. He dug her in the side with his elbow to wake her. 'Would you mind gittin' off me?'

'*Mi amor*,' she cooed. The bed creaked as she rolled over and snuggled into him, her pudgy fingers possessive upon him. 'You certainly know how to satisfy a lady.'

'Do I?' He looked down at her. She had her eyes closed, a cherubic smile on her face above the several chubby chins. 'Did I?'

Slaughter groaned and reached a hand to his whiskey-pounding head. Gradually it came back to him as if through a haze. Eusebio and his pal had produced guitars and started yelling some wild serenade as Dorothea whirled her skirts and did a finger-clicking flamenco dance with Ben, who stomped his heels and pirouetted like a bull-fighter about her. The wine, rum and whiskey had worked its tricks. Slaughter had grabbed hold of Maria and dragged her into the fray to swing her around. 'Trust me to wanna be the life and soul of the party.'

He vaguely remembered that finally Maria had carried him more or less bodily up the stairs and hurled him onto the big, canopy-covered bed. She had ripped off his boots and his pants and tumbled in on top of him without a by-your-leave. Well, he guessed he didn't put up much opposition. It had been a long time. She was like a water-hole in the desert and, even if she came mammoth size, Maria was no amateur at the game.

'My head! How's about a cawfee?'

'Afterwards.' She seemed reluctant to leave the warm bed. 'You gonna be a good boy, Colonel?'

'*Colonel*?' Fat she might be, but Maria certainly knew how to use her fingers to stimulating effect, even with a hangover like his. 'Who told ya that?'

'Oh, they said thass what you tol' Señor Jesus Serrano. I never been in bed with colonel before.'

'Aw, that was a bluff. I was tryin' to impress him. It obviously didn't work. I promoted myself by one word. Nope, I was just a humble loo-tenant, not Lootenant Colonel.'

'You fight in war?'

'Yup. I was raised in Noo Mexico. I was sixteen when I volunteered. I didn't know no better. Jined Wharton's Texas Brigade and went to Kentucky. I was twenty-two by the time I got out, but, I tell ya, I felt like a hundred.'

He lay silent as he remembered.

Too much death, too much random slaughter, men, horses, trampled in the mud. After a while a man almost became immune to it. The corpses of soldiers lying in a ditch as they galloped past might just have been so many dead hogs.

'It had its excitin' moments,' he sighed, as he fondled her dark hair on his chest. 'That man Forrest was a demon. He never wanted to give in. He was born for victory. Five years after it had all begun we covered the retreat back through Alabama. I can see him now, his face and uniform covered in blood, sabre in hand, standing in the stirrups, leading a suicidal charge against the enemy as they crossed the Alabama River and came into Selma. But all we had left were old men and boys. It was like a tidal wave we couldn't stop. We all knew it was over.'

Was she listening? No; what did she care? He was really speaking to himself, trying to make some sense of it. Wasn't Maria the sort of woman he needed to settle down with? A nice, fat, comfortable one, who knew how to cook, who knew how to love, who knew about a man's desires. A real woman. One who would pop out babies like peas from a pod and tend them, devotedly. A woman of flesh and blood. Not some snooty-nosed, pale-skinned, blue-blooded virgin who thought herself too good for him.

To forget, Slaughter pulled the brown-skinned peasant woman up on top of him. She smiled down, cheekily breathing hard, and slapped his face with her mounds of breasts, half-burying him. He caught hold of a nipple in his teeth, and hauled himself up into her reams of flesh, up into her haven of delight. 'Ai-yi-yee! *Caramba!*' she cried. '*Si, si, si!*'

When she had waddled off to fetch him coffee, and served him breakfast of ham and eggs in bed, she wanted to start again. Finally they lay sated, covered in sweat.

Why couldn't he be content, he wondered, to live with a woman like Maria? He knew he never could be.

'You ever bin married, Colonel?' she asked, shyly.

'Yup. I got married to a gal when I was sixteen, before I went off to the war. She promised to wait for me.'

'What happened to her?'

'You really wanna know? It ain't a pretty story.'

'*Si*, I wanna know.'

'You see, it took a while, after the defeat, to git mustered out. I hadn't writ to her for a while. Mebbe she thought I wasn't coming back. I had to cross the Big River and git hold of a hoss to make my way through Texas and Comanche country. Finally I got back to my village of White Oaks, which was close to Fort Stanton.'

'Your wife,' she murmured, snuggled under his arm. 'She was still there?'

'She was still there, all right. I rode into what had once been my father's farm and walked into the house. And there she was — in bed with some blue-belly officer.'

'Jesu Maria! What happened?'

'He made a lunge for his revolver which was hanging from the bedpost. I shot him between the eyes.'

'What about your wife?'

'She was screaming and protesting. I guess it weren't her fault. The gal was lonesome. She had to survive. But some terrible agony came over me. It was like I was in a dream. I shot again. I killed her, too.' He leaned over and picked up the Schofield, staring at it. 'This is the gun I used. I still got it.'

Maria stayed silent for a while, looking up at him, fearfully — the gaunt, stone face, the black hair wreathed about his head, hanging almost to his powerful shoulders. She wriggled free and rolled out of bed, hurriedly pulling on her pantalettes and dress. 'I better go. I gotta help Georgio.'

'Yeah, you run along.'

At the door, Maria paused and asked,

'What happened? To you?'

Slaughter shrugged. 'I gave myself up. If it had been a military court I'd have been strung up. But I was a civilian now and no Southern jury was gonna convict a returning hero soldier-boy for killing a hated Yankee and his whore. They brought in a verdict of justifiable homicide, with a thousand-dollar fine. Satisfied? You did ask.'

'*Si*, I am satisfied,' Maria murmured. 'I am sorry, *señor*. You have had a bad life.'

'Yeah, I guess I have,' he muttered when she was gone. It was the first time he had spoken about it to anyone. It was as if he had been carrying that bag of guilt around on his shoulders for years and it had finally burst. It was like a catharsis. He suddenly felt free, like a man must feel after confessing to a priest.

'That's when I became a bounty hunter,' he said to himself. 'To pay that damn fine.'

He had gone to Silver City where a gang of rustlers had been helping themselves to honest ranchers' stock. He had stalked them into the mountains, killed six of them. There was $200 each on their heads.

Once started on that path it was not easy to stop. He had become judge, jury and executioner. It was as if all feeling had gone. He was like a killing automaton, without mercy. Perhaps that was why he was so successful at his job?

Some of the army officers' friends had vowed to get him, so from Silver City he crossed the mountains into Arizona Territory, which was under the scourge of the Apache and almost as dangerous as Kentucky and Tennessee had been. He learned to survive, travelling on from town to town. Bounty hunting paid well.

Whenever he had to go in and take a man, or men, at gunpoint, he thought of his wife and the Union officer in that bed and a cold fury possessed him.

He preferred it if they fought back. He didn't want to make arrests, get involved with the legal rigmarole. The authorities frowned on him, anyway. It was more satisfying to spill blood, get it over with. Sometimes, he thought, he had been sent there by some Higher Power to clean up these scum, to burn out these nests of rats.

'It ain't a purty profession,' he muttered, as he spun the Schofield's cylinder. 'I gotta git outa this killin' game.'

★ ★ ★

He saddled Cal and rode out into the hills on his own. He had found his old, wide-brimmed hat, lost in the fight with Serrano's men. He was fond of it. It fitted perfectly to shield his eyes, and he had moulded the brim just to his liking. With that on his head, the Schofield on his thigh, the high-powered Lightning back in the saddle-blanket behind him, he felt more in command. Maria had made a clay cast for his left ankle, which had set solid like plaster, from which his bare toes peeped. How he had managed to dance on the ankle he did not know, but a man could do anything when he was drunk! Anyhow, it felt a lot more comfortable. The pinto knew his every touch and command and surged forward beneath him. He, too, seemed to be glad to be back with the man he knew, and eager to please. Horses, like humans, wanted to know where they stood.

Slaughter climbed the pinto high into the Organ Pipe Mountains, which was an apt enough name because they were covered in a forest of strange cacti like organ pipes. He was on the qui vive for Jesus Serrano's *bandidos*, although he figured they wouldn't be back just yet. It was fifty miles or more to the border over extremely rough country. It would take him a couple of days to trail his cattle down there, possibly a day to sell them and recruit more *hombres*, and a day or more to ride back. But, in any event, it was good to be out on his own, with just the horse for company. And it was best to be ready for them.

He rode at an easy pace all day until the sun began to sink into its yellow haze. He sat his pinto and stared out over the desert and rock wasteland. The only living thing in sight was a vulture that circled low in the darkening air, as if watching and waiting for him.

He watched the sun die in agony on the knife points of mountains, in a gesticulation of bloody rays. In its crimson backwash he found a declivity in the rock, made a small fire of mesquite twigs, and cooked up a sidewinder he had shot. He rolled up in his blanket, but the yellow light of the moon, and bad dreams, kept bringing him awake, his hand going to the Colt Lightning between his knees.

The next morning he kept watch for a while from a high vantage point, then returned to the hacienda to be greeted by surprising news. Ben Turner had asked Señor Serrano for his daughter's hand in marriage. It so happened that a priest from a distant village had been making the rounds of his vast parish on his *burro*, giving communion to the Hispanic population, baptizing babies, comforting the sick, and saying prayers over the dead. He had been drummed in to perform the marriage ceremony.

'What's the hurry?' Slaughter asked. 'She's only a kid, barely sixteen. You sure you doing the right thing?'

'I'm sure,' Ben said. 'So's she. We would like you to be our best man.'

'We want to be united in the eyes of God,' Dorothea murmured, hanging onto his arm. 'We want to know what love is like — just in case we are torn apart.'

'Jesus Serrano's going to have some tough *hombres* with him,' Ben said. 'You never know what might happen.'

'He is, and you don't. OK, let's do it.'

The solemn ceremony was the excuse for another wild party with guitars thrumming, and much feasting and drinking. Ben sat with Dorothea on his knee and asked, 'Haven't you ever been wed?'

'Yeah. She was sixteen, too.' Slaughter made a wry grimace. 'It didn't work out. But that don't mean yours won't.'

He offered the newly-weds the master bedroom and they retired early amidst much ribaldry from Eusebio and his pal. Maria went with them to fix up clean sheets. She and Georgio had decided to stay and face whatever happened with their old master. Under the effects of another bottle of brandy, Slaughter had the urge again and tried to entice her to bed with him.

'No!' Maria backed away, crossing herself. 'You kill your wife. You are truly one of the damned.'

'Waal,' he grinned, bemusedly, to himself. 'She's got a point, I s'pose.' Sometimes, it seemed, since the war his life had been like one long, slow suicide, as if he *wanted* to get killed. Well, whatever, it was a miracle he had survived so long. The odds against him were stacked high. One of these days a bullet was bound to get him. The trouble was that he wasn't so sure now that he wanted to die.

'Jeez,' he said, refilling his glass. 'This whiskey sure makes me feel morbid.'

14

The waiting for Serrano to arrive was the hard part. Everybody was on a knife edge. Slaughter occupied himself making sure all the doors and windows were barricaded, that hand guns and rifles were well oiled and that there was plenty of ammunition in readiness. In the nights he took his turn on guard on the roof. Poking around the cellars he found a box of the new-fangled dynamite and fuse wire. He had had plenty of experience blowing up railroads in the war, but in those days they had had to use bulky barrels of gunpowder. He scratched his head and wondered how he might cook up a surprise for Serrano.

Eventually, the longest wait had to end. On the fifth morning they were roused by a shrill hollering in the distance and, running out onto the veranda, they saw Curly coming galloping his pony towards them, shouting and screaming for all he was worth. His hat brim was bent back by the breeze and he was quirting his bronc from side to side as he raced down from the ridge towards the *hacienda*. You would have thought the Apache were after him.

But it wasn't the Apache: it was Jesus Serrano and more than thirty men in tall sombreros, showing in silhouette on the ridge and charging down after the fleeing cowboy.

'Come *on*,' Dorothea urged. 'You can make it.'

Curly was pounding across the bare ground. He had nearly made it. He was through the gateway of the *rancho*. He was forty feet from the house when a rifle shot cracked out. Curly kicked up his boots and arms as the bullet hit him in the back. He tumbled from the saddle and rolled towards them. He looked up at them, his face straining, one open hand raised, pleading. 'They're coming,' he gasped out.

'Yeah.' Slaughter raised his Lightning, aimed carefully, and took one of the racing men out of the saddle, as Ben and Dorothea jumped down to help the cowboy. 'Leave him,' he snapped, levering another slug into the breech. 'He's finished. Git back in the house.'

They scrambled inside and slammed the door shut, barring it with a solid crosspiece. As a precaution Slaughter had brought his pinto and a couple of the mustangs into the house, stabling them in the banqueting room in case the *bandidos* tried to steal them. So there was something akin to bedlam as Ben Turner and Francisco Serrano took up positions at the window ports, back and front, while Maria and Dorothea kept the ammunition ready.

Slaughter shouted to Eusebio and Rodrigo to get up on the western side flat roof, as already arranged, and caught hold of Georgio, dragging him up to the eastern side. 'Curly's dead.

You got to help me and Hank. Keep an eye on the back and down below in case they try to sneak up. You know how to load these thangs?'

'*Si, señor*,' Georgio replied, taking the carbine with a trembling hand.

The *vaquero* arrivals were galloping their horses round and around the hacienda, shooting from the saddle, like the Apaches' disorganized form of warfare, and whooping like them.

When two of them raced their mustangs right up to the front of the house to fire up at the gunports, yelling like maniacs, Slaughter and Hank soon put a stop to that, putting slugs in their chests and knocking them off their saddles and into the Other World.

Down below, Ben or Francisco had got lucky, too, aiming their rifles from the ports and sending one of the Mexicans spinning from his saddle as he raced by.

Soon Jesus Serrano began to see that he was getting nowhere. He called out to his men to dismount and take cover behind the outer wall, while one of them gathered the mustangs and took them back out of gunfire for safety. The battle then developed into an out and out shooting match of rapid fire, but without doing much damage to either side. It was fast becoming a stalemate.

'The question is, how long can we hold out?' James Slaughter growled, lying low on the roof and peering through one of the ports at the front, waiting for a man to show himself so he could take a pot-shot. 'And what are these monkeys gonna git up to soon as it gits dark?'

He looked across at Hank when there was no response. He was lying on his back, the red hole of a bullet entry in his forehead. One of the Mexican marksmen's bullets must have penetrated the port hole and found its billet. 'Hank's gotten unlucky,' Slaughter called back to Georgio. 'You better come over and give me a hand at the front. That's where most of 'em is.'

The chubby Georgio clambered up from his knees, but as soon as he did so a bullet came whining across the roof. *Pa-dow*! He was catapulted backwards over the gunwale to land below in a horse trough.

Slaughter glanced back. 'Where the hell's he gawn? This is lookin' bad.' Angrily he started firing again, emptying the cylinder of his Lightning and had the satisfaction of seeing one of his manstoppers put a hole in the chest of another *vaquero*. 'Mebbe it's time for drastic measures?'

But he was surprised to see a white shirt tied to a carbine being waved, and a man walking forwards. It was Jesus Serrano. 'Hold your fire,' Slaughter shouted. 'Let's hear what he has to say.'

Serrano kept coming. He had taken his own shirt off to act as a flag, and showed a fine, bronzed physique. He was hatless, sweat gleaming, trickling from his grizzled grey curls. His teeth flashed in a reckless grin as he took up a stance some forty paces away. He was wearing a gunbelt around the narrow waist of his black leather trousers, the feet of his silver-toed boots solidly splayed on the sand. 'You know you ain't got a chance,' he shouted.

'That's jest your opinion,' Slaughter hollered back, and he heard Eusebio and Rodrigo hurling insults from the other side of the domed roof.

'I ain't interested in you, Slaughter. You can go. This is between me and him' — he pointed a finger at the front door — 'Francisco Serrano. You shouldn't listen to what he says. He's a liar, a cheat, a thief and a murderer. He killed my father and stole this *estancia*. That is why I took it back.'

'Oh, yeah? And how about pizening Miss Turner's wells? That's what I'm here about.'

'Ach, that's nothing to do with it. She got me mad, that's all. I'll have this out with Francisco Serrano, if he's got the guts. Then I'll make my peace with her.'

'Why don't you have it out with a man your equal with guns? Like me, for instance. I'll willingly step down and meet you.'

'Go talk to Francisco, see what the coward says. When this is decided between him and me we'll call it quits.'

'Ain't no calling it quits far as you and me are concerned. I got a bad foot and some painful ribs to remind me of that.'

'Come quickly.' Dorothea had run up to the roof and was tugging at his sleeve. 'My father is determined to go out and meet him. You've got to stop him.'

'Is it true what Jesus Serrano says?'

'There was some trouble between his father and my father, that's all I know. There was a fight and my father shot him down. But this place belonged to my father. He was the older one.'

'Let's go see. Keep your head down.'

When he got down into the cool shade of the house Francisco was pushing Ben aside, and unbarring the front door. 'Get out of my way, Ben. He can't call me a coward.'

Slaughter caught hold of him. 'What the hell you doin'? He's fast as a rattler. He'll cut you down.'

'This is between me and him.' Francisco drew himself up, stroking back his mane of grey hair, fixing his sombrero, taking a pearl-handled revolver from his gunbelt, cocking it, spinning the cylinder to make sure it was fully-loaded. 'He has insulted me for long enough. I am no coward.' He returned the revolver to the holster, and pulled open the heavy door. He pushed Dorothea away as she begged and pleaded with him. He offered his hand to Ben. 'If the worst happens, look after my daughter.'

He patted Dorothea's shoulder and smiled at her, proudly. 'Don't worry. I am not afraid any more. It is time to be a man.'

Don Francisco stepped out onto the veranda and stared at his nephew. 'So, I am ready for you. You had better be ready to eat your words or defend yourself.'

A crafty smile spread over Jesus Serrano's face. 'Come forward. What shall we make it? Thirty paces? I should have done this a long time ago.'

'Whatever you wish. Thirty paces is good enough.'

There was a hush of silence among the watching men as he stepped down onto the sand into the harsh sunlight and strode forward. In spite of his fine costume he looked a frail man against his powerfully built opponent. 'Is this far enough?'

'Sure, that's fine,' Jesus smiled, tossing the carbine aside, and patting the revolver pig-stringed to his thigh. 'I prefer a carbine, but this'll have to do. We wanna play fair, don't we?'

'We do, you scoundrel. Defend yourself!' As he angrily shouted the words Francisco snatched the pearl-handled gun out of its holster. But his hurry was such he aimed badly. There was a roar of explosion and a flash of flame and the bullet cut through his nephew's shirt sleeve as he rolled aside onto the dust and snatched up the carbine.

Francisco turned on him and fired again. But Jesus Serrano was too fast for him. Lying on the sand he pumped three shots into the older man making him spin and dance with shock. Francisco slowly collapsed into the dust and lay bleeding, profusely, his mouth gaping open, his eyes staring.

'That weren't fair, you cur,' Slaughter growled. He had stepped out onto the veranda to watch. 'Thirty paces favours a carbine.'

'He shoulda thought of that.'

Slaughter had his Schofield out and ready, but Jesus Serrano had already started pumping shots his way, backed by the *vaqueros* behind the wall. Slaughter only had time to wing off a couple of slugs that went wide as Serrano scrambled away. Bullets splintered into the door about their heads and he pushed Dorothea and Ben back into the house, backing in after them, still firing. He slammed the door shut. 'That hyena. I knew you couldn't trust him.'

Dorothea was sobbing as if her heart would break. 'What about my father? We can't leave him there.'

'He's dead, honey. He knew the score.'

The battle had commenced again outside. Those still alive inside took up their stations on the roof and downstairs, except for Slaughter. He glanced out of a porthole, and shook his head as he noted that most of the men were stationed along the outer wall. Just where he wanted them. 'They've asked for it,' he grunted, as he knelt down and examined a plunger that was linked to a fuse wire. 'This better work.'

He had spent considerable time digging trenches to guide the wire out under the front yard at about a foot below ground, and spreading connecting wires to various spots along the outer wall. He wasn't familiar with this new-fangled battery operation but he hoped he had got it right. 'Here we go,' he shouted. 'Let's blow the varmints to hell.'

Those in the house paused for seconds and peered out. Suddenly the buried dynamite exploded. *Pow! Pow! Pow!* There were shouts and screams as men were thrown into the air, the bloody hands and legs of their dismembered bodies splattering down to the ground. When the smoke cleared others were seen climbing out of the dust, unsteady and shaken, looking around for their comrades.

'How they like that?' Slaughter muttered. 'It's a pity I ain't fixed up no more.'

He estimated that more than ten of the *vaqueros* must have been killed by the explosions. Others were wounded, lying groaning on the sand. The rest were running back to their horses and, urged on by Serrano, were climbing into the saddles to go charging about the house, to attack from all sides.

'Hang on,' Slaughter muttered, after the battle had resumed for another half-hour. 'I cain't see no sign of that monkey. I figure he's high-tailed it out of here.'

'Who?' Eusebio asked.

'Jesus Serrano. Who else? I gotta git after him. But how the hell am I goin' to git outa here?'

15

The three cowboys were kneeling over a wild, full-grown bull they had cut from the bawling herd, two of them holding him down by his horns and haunches, the other taking a Mexican Hat branding iron from the fire to hiss red-hot on his hide. They did not notice the man on the white stallion come riding out of the rocky landscape and go splashing across the Rio Diablo.

'Where 'n hell's he going?' Fat Bob said, uneasily, when he saw him. He was busy cutting up chunks of beef for the men's supper on the tailboard of the chuckwagon. 'What's happened to the others?'

He watched Jesus Serrano go loping past, the silver-buckled gunbelt around his waist, the lavishly engraved six-gun in his holster, the Spencer seven-shot carbine in the saddle boot. A powerful man on a powerful horse. The flash of silver on spurs, silver-toed boots, bridle, the conchos decorating his sombrero. A dark, grim-faced man. An avenger.

Fat Bob watched him ride on across the river grass. He was heading in the direction of the ranch. Miss Rose was there alone, apart from old Jed, the farrier. Maybe he ought to go warn the boys, go after him?

Fat Bob swallowed his guilt, his fear. What chance would he have against a fast gun like Serrano? Or the other three? They were middle-aged men, 'punchers, not shootists. 'It ain't none of our business,' he muttered, and hammered his cleaver into the beef. Fat Bob was too fond of his food, his sleep, and, he figured, he wasn't paid enough to toss his life away. 'Mebbe he's jest making a social call,' he muttered. 'Used to be sweethearts, didn't they? He ain't likely to hurt her.'

★ ★ ★

Rose Turner had thought she heard the rumble of thunder, and looked up at the sky over the mountain peaks. No, hardly a cloud in the sky. It was oppressively hot, like the calm before the storm. No, no sign of rain. Maybe it hadn't been thunder? Maybe it had been the rumble of gunfire?

How long now had Ben and the others been gone? This was the fifth day, surely? Rose did not like being alone in the ranch house. It was eerie, especially at nights, lying in bed listening to the chorus of the coyotes shrilling, or, perhaps, a grey wolf baying at the moon. So lonesome, so savage, they sounded. Rose bolted the doors and shuttered the windows, kept the Winchester rifle handy, and the Dragoon revolver under her pillow. She started awake at every unusual sound. There was only old Jed, the wagoner, on the ranch and he was across the way in the bunk house, and, anyway, wouldn't be much use. The long nights reminded Rose of the days of her girlhood when the Apache were on the prowl. Every full moon brought terror.

Rose had berated Ben for taking half their men to the Rancho Tejon to join Slaughter, but she began to wish she had gone with them. What could have happened? As the seconds ticked by, the days and nights passed, this question obsessed her.

To take her mind off things she had gone to look for the old Indian, Brave Night, who lived in a tumbledown shack on the edge of town and was tolerated because of his so-called healing 'magic'. There were a good many white folk who visited him after dark. White-haired, his face grooved and eroded, he was supposed, too, to be able to divine water. Rose decided to put him to the test. The old man started off at the poisoned well, and wandered away for miles across the hills, occasionally pausing to start some kind of mournful chant, and wave a green cottonwood stick around in his hands. Rose had begun to tire of his antics. He was probably just putting on a show for the silver dollar she had given him. But suddenly his crooning stopped, the switch in his hands began to jump and quiver. He pointed to the ground and said, 'Water here. Plenty good.'

Their finances were not good, but it was worth a gamble. Rose had visited the copper mine near the town and agreed with the company boss to hire, at an exorbitant rate, heavy digging equipment. A big, suspended pile-driver hammer on a tall platform drove a steel pipe deep into the ground. The men had arrived to start work at the chosen spot.

Rose had been relieved to see the dawn this day, and invited Jed over to have breakfast with her before they busied themselves with their chores around the ranch. All through the afternoon she listened to the thudding of the rig in the distance, and felt jumpy and uneasy for some reason. She was bathing in the wash house when she thought she heard a sound, the whickering of a horse, out in the yard. She quickly began to pull her clothes on over her wet body. Her heart was beating fast. She had left her father's guns in the living-room. Anyone who has tried dressing when they are wet will know how difficult it was. Her lace-trimmed pantalettes stuck to her thighs as she tried to jerk them up. Her blouse caught on her damp elbows. The more she hurried in her panic the more difficult it became. She wrapped on her Mexican skirt and, barefoot, creaked open the bath-house door, peering inside the house. There was her Dragoon over on the table. She looked out into the yard beyond but could not see anybody.

'Perhaps I'm imagining things,' she murmured.

'You ain't imagining nothing.' His husky voice spoke in her ear, and his hand covered her mouth as she screamed. Her right arm was being twisted up behind her, and his knee was between her thighs. 'Maybe I will snap your beautiful neck.'

He spun her around and slapped her hard across her jaw, sending her sprawling to the floorboards, and slithering halfway across the room. Her head was spinning as she tried to get to her feet, but his fist was in her hair, almost pulling it from the roots, and he had her back across his knee. Serrano's dark face split in a flashing grin. 'Or maybe I will let you live. What's it to be, my lovely? You going to come easy?'

For answer Rose tried to twist and scramble away from him, even though he was hanging onto her hair and the pain was excruciating. She managed to reach a vase on the table and smashed it across his head. For reply he backhanded her with his hard, gloved fist, knocking her sprawling across the floor again.

'You wan' it the hard way, you wild bitch?' He was kneeling on her, holding her thighs together, like he might a struggling longhorn, grinning at her, grabbing hold of both her wrists in one large hand and whipping a piece of cord around them, tying her hands tight. 'This time I am not giving you any chances, *señorita*. Soon to be *señora* when we get to Mexico.'

'You wouldn't. I'm not going to marry you. You're out of your mind. Leave me alone, you pig,' she screamed at him. 'I hate you. You disgust me. Just *go*. Forget me.'

'How can I forget you, *mi amor*? You promised yourself to me, remember? Now, get on your damn feet.' He dragged her up, ripping her blouse. It fell free across her shoulder, revealing her pale skin. 'Get moving, honey.'

'No! Jesus, don't, please!' Blood trickled from her full lower lip as she pleaded with him. 'I can't go. I have no boots.'

'Here.' He threw her into the rocker, kicked them to her. 'Put them on. We got a long ride. And here.' He tossed her a thick poncho and her straw Stetson. 'Take these. I want to keep you in good shape for our bridal night.'

'You're mad.' She pulled the boots on with her bound hands. And glanced at the revolver on the table, the Winchester leaned close by. 'You can't force me to marry you.'

'Can't I? In Mexico we have a different set of rules. The woman does what she's told.' He smiled as he saw her looking at the guns. 'Don't even think about it. If I have to, I'll kill you. Remember that.'

He jerked her to her feet, thrust the poncho over her head and shoulders, the hat on her head and, his fingers gripping the nape of her neck, pushed her roughly out of the screen door onto the veranda.

'Howdy!' The town sheriff, Moses Murdoch, was riding towards them, cantering in across the dusty yard. 'Where ya off to, Miss Turner? I been out collecting country taxes an' you seem to have forgot yours is due.'

He reined in his bronco and blinked at her in the shade of the canopy, the tall, dark man, with the piercing eyes, and grizzled curls, stood behind her. 'You two goin' somewhere?'

'Get out of here,' Serrano said. 'Call for your taxes some other day.'

'Sheriff, do something,' Rose screamed, trying to struggle free. 'He's kidnapping me.'

Serrano held on to her by her back hair. He had the Spencer carbine in his right hand and he dug it hard into her back. 'Shut up! Don't take no notice what she says, Murdoch. This is 'tween her and me. You've had your payments regular, haven't you?'

'You can't do this Mr Serrano,' the sheriff protested. There were patches of sweat on the shirt taut across his fat belly. And perspiration was trickling into his eyes. 'I don't mind lookin' t'other way over a bit of rustling, but kidnappin' a white woman; thass a federal offence. You better think twice.'

Whether, in his nervousness, after he had wiped the sweat from his eyes, Moses Murdoch was merely going to hitch up his pants, or whether he was going for the Colt on his thigh, Rose never knew. Serrano didn't wait to find out. He fired the carbine one-handed. Flame, smoke and lead barked out, pitching the sheriff from his horse. Murdoch lay on the sand, his blood and life oozing away. He gave a little cry of agony as he expired. 'You should'n — '

'That's the final payment,' Serrano hissed. Old Jed had come running bow-legged from the wagon shed. Serrano aimed the carbine at him. 'You want the same treatment?'

Jed tottered to a halt, looked apologetically at Rose, and laid his rifle on the sand. 'What you gonna do with her?'

'Guess. She's gonna get what she deserves. So, get her horse saddled, and two spares from the corral. *Pronto*!'

When this was done, under Serrano's

watchful eye, keeping one hand on her nape, the Spencer prodding her ribs, he ordered her to mount up. 'Sling your leg across. We don't stand on ceremony.' He grinned up at her as he ordered Jed to tie her ankles to the stirrups. 'You're gonna have to spread 'em for me soon enough.'

The Mexican whacked his quirt across her gelding's rear quarters, setting him off. He touched spurs to his white stallion and raced after her, drawing alongside and, in front, leading the spare mustangs. When he reached the rocks and cacti of the hillside he attached a leading rein from one of the mustangs to her horse. 'Remember, you just follow me along. If you try to get away I'll shoot your horse down. Then I'll kill you. But, before I do that, guess what I'm going to do.'

Serrano grinned, recklessly. He adjusted his sombrero, put the carbine in the boot, and rode off at a steady lope, following a trail through the hills he seemed to know, leading them in his wake, forcing Rose to hang on as best she could with her hands bound, eating his dust.

★ ★ ★

James Slaughter saw the buzzards circling over Mexican Hat from half a mile away and his heart fell. He urged his pinto on at a hard lope. Serrano's stallion had more power and speed, but Cal had a big heart and great endurance. He would go 'til he dropped. He figured Serrano had an hour on him. Anything could have happened in that time.

'Hey, *amigos*,' Eusebio had called out to the *bandidos* after beckoning them forward for a pow-wow. 'Why you keep shooting at us? We got nothing you want. Your boss, he has hight-tailed it. He won't be coming back. Who's going to pay you for risking your necks? Why don't you go back to where you come from? You not wanted here.'

Eusebio had shot the hat off one of the Mexicans just to reinforce his argument, and watched them as they withdrew to discuss this. It looked like they were packing up to go. Slaughter took his chance and sent his pinto skittering out of the back door. The *bandidos* watched him go haring away towards the Rio Diablo. If they had known he had a thousand bucks in his back pocket they would probably have given chase.

Slaughter saw the sheriff lying on the sand in a pool of blood, flies insistently buzzing, ants making a start on his eyes. 'Hold it right there, you varmint,' old Jed shouted, his rifle trained on him through a window of the ranch house.

'I'm on your side,' Slaughter shouted. 'Where's Rose?'

'He took her,' Jed whined. 'I couldn't do nuthin'. He had me covered, using her as a shield. He went thataway' — he pointed east — 'with two spare hosses along.'

At that point an old Indian arrived,

running up, excitedly, to tell them, 'We find water. Not good water. Bad water.' He waved his arms to show how it had whooshed up in a fountain. 'Black water. Deep down.'

'Black water. You mean oil. That's no good to nobody, is it? You any good at tracking?'

'I fight many years with Cochise,' Brave Night said. 'The uncle of Geronimo.'

'Sounds good. There's ten dollars for you if you help me find Miss Turner. She's been snatched. And it don't look good. If Serrano's ready to kill a lawman he's ready to kill anyone. He's gone mad dog.'

'I help you.' The ancient Apache had a headband around his long white hair, a shirt and dusty cavalry jacket, the tails of a loin-cloth hanging between his sun-blackened legs. He wore knee-length moccasins. 'The soldiers no lock me up because I am old, have many years. But I got plenty life in me. Eyes like hawk. I help you.'

'Good. Go git yourself a horse and saddle.'

'I no need saddle,' Brave Night said. 'Saddle no good.'

'Jest git on with it, will ya? We're wastin' time. Jed, git me some dried jerky for a coupla days an' coffee beans. I'll fill the canteens.'

Maybe it was a good idea of Serrano's to take spare horses, to ride them alternately, give his own a rest? Maybe it wasn't? They would be bound to slow him up.

'Right,' he shouted across to the Indian in the corral. 'Don't take all day about choosing one. Let's go.'

★ ★ ★

He had been wondering whether taking Brave Night was a good idea, or not. As the night began to close over them he decided it was. He might be old but the Apache appeared to know what he was doing, spotting sign on the hard, rocky ground that Slaughter would have surely missed, and sweeping his hand, pointing forward. 'They go this way.'

It looked as if Serrano and his captive were heading for Tucson the hard way, cutting through a web of bare mountains through which few men knew their way. In the sudden darkness of the desert land after the sun had gone and before the moon rose, Slaughter decided to keep going along an arroyo the trail had been leading through in the hope of catching up. But after another hour of darkness he called a halt. He didn't want to miss any tracks. In this maze of mountains there was no knowing which way Serrano might turn. It was barely visited, let alone mapped.

He fretted at the delay and tried not to think what the young woman might be going through. All he knew was a determination to catch up. Brave Night had lit a small fire and they chawed on the jerky and dried biscuits, pounded beans for coffee. The horses could do with rest. They gave them a handful of corn and cupfuls of water, and hitched them to loose graze among the thorns.

'Best git some sleep,' he said. 'I'll take first watch.' He wouldn't put it past Serrano doubling back, or trying to ambush them. He was as crafty as a snake.

They set off at dawn's first light, keeping their eyes peeled, but, after travelling most of the day, they had still not caught sight of the fugitive. Brave Night studied tracks. 'He go this way.'

'How long ago?'

The Indian shrugged, raised his palm, fingers outstretched. 'Five hours, maybe.'

'That's not good. He's pushing hard.'

The sun was bleeding away into the mountains at their backs as they descended to the small, cathedral-like church of San Xavier del Bac, known as the dove of the desert. The sun's rays were flushing its adobe bricks a luminous crimson.[1] With its towers, its pillars and parapets, and ornately carved front, the baroque mission church standing alone in the desert was an architectural gem. But no priest was in residence. Since the Apache wars it had been deserted.

Strangely enough, a tribe of Papago Indians had chosen to live in their beehive-shaped huts around this symbol of alien culture imposed upon them.

'They worship Boboquivari,' Brave Night said, pointing across the serene distances of the basin beyond the church to the more than 6,000-foot peak dominating the border mountains.

'Ask 'em if they seen anyone.' As he watched Brave Night ease his mustang over to the thatched huts of the Papagos, who had generally

---

[1] The blinding white stucco of this church today is a more recent addition.

lived peacefully with the white man, and in fear of the Apache, he studied the white-dust trail winding back north towards Tucson, and another going east to Tombstone. He was pretty sure Serrano would have taken the trail south towards Nogales on the border, and safety.

Brave Night confirmed this when he returned.

'A man and white woman go that way about three hours ago. She is tied to horse, but she look OK.'

'Three hours? How far is it to the border? Forty miles? We gotta git after them.'

'The horses come long way. They need rest.'

'Yeah, we'll set off at midnight. Let's brew up coffee.'

They sat and watched the Papagos doing a shuffling dance in the sun's afterglow, waving their arms towards the big mountain. 'What 'n hell they wailing about?'

'They do rain dance. They beg the

mountain for rain.'

'Fat lotta good that'll do.'

'Who knows? Maybe magic work, maybe not. Good magic, bad magic. You got to have the power. White man no understand.'

'No, maybe not. But I'm quarter-breed and I don't believe it. You get what you go after in this world. Not what you pray for.'

'Maybe,' Brave Night grunted, as he squatted. He looked, fearfully, up at the great mountain. 'Maybe not.'

16

'Damn! It's that lousy sage rat.' Serrano had taken a brass telescope from his saddle-bag and was intently studying the trail behind them. They had been travelling all day, but every time he had looked behind he had seen the spiral of dust kicked up by James Slaughter and the Indian. And they had gradually gained on them. The white stallion had got over-heated and was suffering from exhaustion. The Mexican was in half a mind to abandon him. The woman looked none too good, come to that, her hair sticking to her damp, pale face, her wrists and ankles swollen and bleeding where the cords had cut into her.

'Come on,' he said, cutting her free, pointing up the mountainside to a cliff overhang where the trail passed through a steep chasm. 'We're going up into them rocks. This time the sonuvabitch is asking for it.'

Rose had had a faint gleam of hope, but now she saw that any horseman passing along the trail below would be easy prey to a marksman up in the rocks. But, what could she do? Through the past two nights as she crouched in her bonds, and Serrano groped her, jeering at her, licking at her, making lewd threats, she had kept him at bay by reminding him that Slaughter would be after him. It had kept him edgy, unwilling to abandon his carbine, lower his guard. But now he had seen that Slaughter was really there, Serrano's eyes had taken on a hunted, demented look. There was no knowing what he might do. So she meekly followed him, easing her wrists, leading the horse, glad, at least, to be on foot, climbing up the steep slope through a ghostly forest of saguaros as the sun set, casting them in shade.

Jesus Serrano seemed determined to

reach the vantage point by going up around through a dry arroyo chiselled deeply into the rocks, scrambling on his way, dragging the poor stallion and the other two horses with him. Rose knew that anthropomorphism was absurd, but it was hard not to see the stately saguaro as a race of sentient creatures standing in the arrested gestures of supplication, command or prayer. Their giant arms were pointed upwards, downwards, sideways, some curled around in apparent embrace, some solitary standing, as if questioning, who were these invaders of their mountain? In the fading light they made her shiver. When she turned to look back at the trail cutting across the great basin, the men following, if men there were, had dropped out of sight behind one of the grey-blue ridges. The steepness and height of their climb made her feel dizzy. She turned to go on.

A great drumroll of thunder startled her. Fork lightning riveted the turquoise night sky above the turret of Boboquivari.

And great blobs of rain began to splash into the dust and patter onto her face. Rose looked up to the peak and saw black clouds rolling down the mountainside in a sinister manner. She braced herself as the air became dark and cold, and the thunder god gave another earth-trembling roar. It truly seemed as if the end of the world was nigh.

'Hurry!' Serrano beckoned to her, urging her on. 'We can make it to that cave before it breaks.'

But he was wrong. Suddenly the whole sky seemed to crack open upon them with a tremendous tearing sound. There were a thousand drummers up in the sky, their crashing roll of sound bouncing off the canyon walls. Instead of being soft and warm, the rain became a pounding deluge. It wasn't rain. It was as if somebody up there was tipping great tubs of water over them, never-ending. Rose screamed as the mustang broke away from her in terror and headed off back down the arroyo. If she had had any sense she would have tried to climb up the steep walls to safety. But, lashed by the rain, her skirt clinging to her, it was all she could do to stay upright. And then she saw the great wall of water coming towards her. They had no time to take avoiding action. The stallion's legs were knocked from under him, and she saw him coming flailing and swirling towards her, passing her, his head outstretched, eyes bulging, as she, too, was swept away.

Rose was drowning, choking, in the muddy six-foot-deep rush of turbulent water, which was fed by all the other little arroyos eroded over millennia, flowing into creeklets, to unite in this powerful river running downhill. She tried, desperately, to reach the smooth sides of the narrow defile, but even when she did so she could not hold on. She was hurled on down by the cascade. Suddenly, though, she was stopped. The breath was knocked out of her as she was rammed up tight against a rock. She hung onto it, and, in a shudder of lightning, saw the two other horses go careering helplessly by in the flood.

Another ball of lightning spun into her eyes and through the intensity of rain and water she saw Jesus Serrano on the far side trying to struggle out of the torrent onto a ledge of rock. He succeeded, and turned to stare at her, his teeth bared in a snarl of effort, like a coyote's. Rose managed, too, to pull herself up onto the rock. And, in another horrendous crash of thunder and vast flash of jagged lightning, she saw that the flood had half-torn her blouse from her, and her breasts, streaming with rain, were naked. Even in such moments of peril she tried to cover herself, but there was nothing she could do.

Suddenly she saw a figure poised on the rock above Serrano, a dark figure, his shoulder-length hair lashed by the rain. Why the bounty hunter did not pull his revolver and shoot, she did not know — some odd sense of honour, perhaps? Instead, he leapt, pitching himself out from the rock, to land, kicking his feet into Serrano's back. He was pelting him with hammer blows, but the Mexican was taking them, throwing him off, fighting back. The two men were struggling and slithering back and forth in the torrential rain. 'Oh, my God!' Rose gasped, as Slaughter slipped and rolled to the water's edge. Serrano was picking up a rock and he cracked it, viciously, against the American's head, tumbling him into the flood.

'No!' Rose screamed, as she saw Slaughter swept away on the flood, and spun in the eddy across to her side. She leaned from her rock to try to catch hold of his hand. For moments their eyes met, but he slipped from her and was swept away. But not far! He was hanging onto a rock as the rush of water tore at his legs.

'Let go!' Rose cried, for she had seen Jesus Serrano get to his feet, and take his revolver from his belt. He was levelling it at the back of the man hanging to the rock across the stream from him. It was an easy shot, but he was making sure he did not miss. 'James,' she screamed, 'go with the flood.' But her voice was lost in the thunder and noise.

Lightning flashed on Serrano's face, showing his snarl of triumph as he savoured the moment, took first pressure on the trigger. But, as he was about to fire, he threw up his hands. Rose saw an arrow sticking from his chest. He was clawing at it, trying to pull it free. Another arrow embedded itself in him and he fell to one knee. Another arrow. And another. He collapsed on the ground, kicking and twisting, and Rose watched, horrified, his death throes.

Even more frightening to her was the sight of the Apache Indian bounding down from the big rock to kneel over Serrano. A knife flashed in his hand, poised high, and he was ripping the curly black scalp from the skull, holding it in triumph to the skies, brandishing it at the brooding crest of Boboquivari, and wailing a lament. Rose's fear turned to surprise as she recognized Brave Night.

Suddenly she was startled by a man standing beside her, a man in wet clothing, his strong arm around her, his rough fingers gripping her nakedness. 'Thank God he didn't kill you,' she murmured, as she nuzzled her head into his shoulder, shivering with cold.

'Aw, they cain't kill me. I got things to do.'

Rose smiled, gratefully, squeezed his hand to her breasts and reached up to kiss his rock face. How long she stood there entwined into him she was not sure. All she knew was a kind of numbness and elation. The violent storm passed over and the rain became drizzle. The Indian had gone. When the torrent in the arroyo subsided to calf-depth she saw him coming back up towards them. 'All their hosses gone or dead,' he said. 'Our'n OK.'

They climbed back down to the trail. The bounty hunter swung onto his pinto, put an arm down to pull her up as if she were no more than a child. He settled her on the saddle across his knees and set the horse cantering back the way they had come. Rose only knew the surging strength of the horse flowing through her, Slaughter's strong arm pulling her tightly to him, closing over her bare breasts as they rode. She trembled with a fear and anticipation. She knew there was nothing she could do to oppose him. It was as if it was all pre-ordained.

17

'*Cursum perficio*,' was inscribed on the headstone of Don Francisco Serrano's grave where they gathered to give him a belated funeral service.

'The Latin means 'My journey is over',' Dorothea explained.

'That's how I feel,' Slaughter said, replacing his hat. 'I've had enough of wandering.'

Ben put his arm around his young wife's waist. 'We are going to run this place the way her father would have wanted us to. How about you, James? Want to be my ramrodder?'

'I been thinkin' of taking Murdoch's place as sheriff of San Andreas. A nice quiet li'l number.'

'Don't be silly.' Rose squeezed his arm and smiled. 'You're my ramrodder now.'

She remembered the strange night

they spent in the church of San Xavier del Bac, beneath its seven dome-shapes, lying on their blankets on the bare floor before the altar. It was blasphemous, she had no doubt, but it was also wonderful to lie there naked under the gaze of St Xavier in his three-cornered hat. The man called Slaughter had been gentle with her at first, but he had also been wild and fierce as she clung to him. It had been good.

In the morning she had half-expected him to ride on his way. But he had sent for a priest from Tucson to marry them.

'It looks like there's money in oil,' Ben said. 'You might get rich.'

'Yeah, thass why I married her, for her money.' Slaughter squeezed Rose's hand as they strolled back to the *hacienda*, pausing to look out over the great basin of their neighbouring ranches. 'Life can be a bitch,' he drawled, his green eyes glimmering in their slits. 'But sometimes it gives ya a break. I figure I've finally got lucky.'